A SECRET FOUNDATION

THE BUILDERS, BOOK 1

VANESSA GRAY BARTAL

DRY CREEK PRESS

*P*ete Samperi sniffed the air. Fall in Brooklyn wasn't always the best time to inhale. He smelled rotting trash, a whiff of fish from the market, burning rubber from a tire fire, and a few hints of decaying leaves. More than that, he smelled change. It was coming as inevitably and surely as it always did.

Maybe "always" was a stretch. Change hadn't come to him too often. A third generation Italian-American, he lived in the same apartment where he had been born, where his father had been born, and where his grandfather had taken his first job as a building superintendent, the job Pete now held. For all of his life the same four blocks of his predominately Italian neighborhood had been exactly the same, as had the neighboring four blocks of the Hassidic Jewish neighborhood on one side and the four blocks of the Puerto Rican neighborhood on the other. But in the last few years, the Puerto Rican side had started to *gentrify*. It was a nice word, if you didn't know what it meant. To rich people coming from Manhattan, it meant getting real estate at a steal. To the people who had lived in those neighborhoods their whole lives, it meant getting run out on a rail because they could no longer afford to live there.

It would happen to his neighborhood, he was certain. The

Manhattan invaders were a scourge, like the immigration done by his grandparents, only in reverse. Instead of poor, unskilled, fresh-off-the-boat foreigners, Brooklyn was now being overrun by white, wealthy over-educated people with an eye for change. Away would go the family-run markets and restaurants—where the fish was as questionable as the server's friendliness. In their stead would come trendy places with cutesy misspellings of their names. Prices of everything would skyrocket. Cabs would start making regular appearances where they had never dared to go. Then the building renovations would begin, all in the name of "progress." First the less-entrenched neighbors would leave, then the families would give up and move to the suburbs. Finally the old people would either die or be moved to retirement villas to wait for death.

The whole business depressed Pete. More than that, it scared him. If it were just him and Marie, they could make it, move somewhere deeper into the Burroughs and start anew. But he was a father now, five times over. All he knew was how to run and repair a building. He didn't want to start over, didn't want to go away.

He stopped in front of his building and tried to think like an investor. It wasn't hard to do. Even a financial dummy could see what a good opportunity it was. A pre-war five story brick with an elevator, the building was loaded with charm and character. Even better, it was a mere four-block walk to the Subway station. Of course there was always the chance that they might keep Pete on as the building's Super, but it was doubtful. From what he had heard, most of the real estate was being snapped up by conglomerates. They got rid of Supers, installed fancy doormen, and hired contracting services to handle repairs.

His wife opened a window and pushed her head through. "Pete, you loafing?"

He walked closer and leaned in for a kiss. "Maybe."

"Why you look so serious? Did something happen?" She gripped his hands.

"No, but something is going to. The neighborhood is changing, Marie."

"Mr. Rossi from the market said another one of the Puerto Rican's building's sold. He said some guys in a fancy car were parked outside taking pictures of his store the other day."

"It's only a matter of time until this place sells."

They were quiet a few beats.

"So we'll move," she said.

"And find somewhere that can fit five kids? We're squeezed in here as it is."

"Remember when we were little and used to play in the hallway on rainy days?" she asked.

"I remember you were too cute for your own good." They had always been together, it seemed. Neighbors and sweethearts from birth.

"You used to talk about moving to the country and getting a horse."

"I was a horse-obsessed kid. Stupid thing for a kid from Brooklyn to be," he said.

"Why? Why's it so stupid? We're gonna move anyway. What if we made a big move, somewhere with fresh air and space for the kids to roam around? Somewhere we could get that horse."

"You wanna leave Brooklyn?"

"If we weren't being squeezed out, then no, this never woulda come up. But, Pete, it's gonna be the same wherever we go. The city is sprawling out. Pretty soon the only place we'll be able to afford will be some place that'll get us or the kids killed. I'm a mother now; I gotta think different. Maybe it's time to give the kids something we never had—land, fresh air, nature."

"But the money…" he started.

"Things don't cost as much outside the city. You know my cousin Trudy in Kentucky? I found out how much her house cost—a hundred thousand, and it has four bedrooms."

Pete whistled, duly impressed. "I guess it's worth looking into, but what'll the kids think?"

"They're kids, they'll love it. What's not to love? Getting a bigger place, some land. It's every child's dream."

"I'll have to learn to drive," Pete said.

"So will I," Marie said. "But if we wait four years, Joe can teach us."

The rate their oldest was going, he would be driving illegally long before his sixteenth birthday. Pete had long been worried about his children—Joe, the consummate oldest brother who felt torn between his desire to misbehave with his friends and his desire to set a good example for his younger siblings. Benedict who, at the age of ten, had yet to misbehave. Jessamine, their lone girl and leader of the pack. Giovanni, bookish, quiet, and steady. And Mossimo, the beloved baby. The neighborhood wasn't the same as it had been when he and Marie were kids. It was getting to the point where he was afraid to let them play outside. Maybe if they moved to the country, their kids would find some nice friends to play with, friends who didn't lift hubcaps for kicks.

Mentally Pete began to calculate how long their savings would last if he quit his job. All he knew how to do was operate a building and fix things. He was good with his hands and handy with a hammer. Was there a need for that in other parts of the country? "Where do we begin?" Pete asked.

"At the beginning," Marie said.

"You have a logical mind, Mrs. Samperi."

"Thank you, Mr. Samperi." She leaned out the window and kissed him once more.

CHAPTER 1

"I want to be set up."

Jessamine Samperi looked down her prominent nose at her younger brother, Giovanni. He was only two years younger, but those two years had always counted for a lot. "You want to be set up? You, Mr. 'I don't need help getting a date' suddenly wants to be set up. Mr. 'I don't like change and uncertainty.' Mr. Precise wants to be set up?"

"Yes, with one of your friends."

"Which one?" Jess asked.

"Vivian."

She regarded him critically, the teasing glint gone from her eyes. "No."

"Why not?"

"Because Vivian is special. She's sweet and sincere; you'll hurt her."

"Have I ever asked you to be set up before?" he said.

"No," she admitted.

"Doesn't that tell you something about my level of intent? Why would I ask to be set up with someone and then hurt her? You're making it sound like I'm Leonardo DiCaprio, like I'm going to take her to my yacht and drop her on an island with a bottle of rum when I tire of her."

She examined him from the top of his tidy black mane to the tips of his polished leather wingtips. With his round tortoiseshell glasses and perfectly pressed chinos, he looked more like an architect than a construction worker. "You're always looking for something better, for something perfect. You'll move on. You'll hurt her. You'll leave her behind. She's too sweet for that."

"She's so fragile that one date with your brother will ruin her life?" Giovanni asked, his voice rising with affront.

"If you only want one date with her, why do you want to be set up?" Jess asked, ever suspicious of all of her brothers. Even Giovanni, with whom she was probably the closest.

"Because I think we could hit it off. Come on, Jess." He laced his fingers together under his chin, pleading.

"No, I like Vivian. I want to continue to be friends with her. It's going to be hard to do if you annihilate her heart."

"Look, I'll make you a deal. We'll go on one casual date to see how things go. If it's not an immediate love match, I'll back off nicely and she'll never see my face again."

She quirked a shapely brow. "One date?"

"One little date. Teensy."

"Casual?"

"So casual we'll go in the morning," he said.

"I'm not sure if a morning date is causal or weird," Jess said.

"Just ask her," he pled.

"All right, but so help me, Giovanni, if you hurt her..."

"Gentle as a lamb, Jess," he promised, holding up his right hand like an oath taker, but inside he could hardly contain his glee. He had met a few of Jess's book club friends in passing a few weeks ago. Since then he hadn't been able to stop thinking about the luscious Vivian. She was exactly the type of woman he was looking for—beautiful, tall, long blond hair, beautiful, killer blue eyes, leggy, beautiful. If Giovanni had sketched his perfect woman, she would look exactly like Vivian.

He could hardly believe it when Jess told him she was single. And now she was agreeing to fix him up with her. He wasn't a big believer in superstition, but he had the funny feeling his life was about to change forever.

CHAPTER 2

"**I** can't believe I'm doing this," Vivian whispered to her reflection for the tenth time that morning. She had never been on a blind date before, and certainly not with someone who looked like Giovanni Samperi. He was, to borrow vernacular from her teenage days, a super hottie. All the Samperis were nice looking, but Vivian had always secretly thought Giovanni was the cutest. And now she had a date with him.

"Breathe," she commanded her reflection. Her hair—thick, long, dark, glossy, and by far her best feature, was not cooperating today. Outside was humid, causing her locks to clump in odd ringlets and lay slack in other places, like a sheepdog after running through a burr patch.

Why are you doing this? Vivian had questioned Jessamine, sure the date must have been some kind of pity invite.

He said he wants to go out with you. He practically begged me to be set up with you.

Vivian hadn't said anything more, but she had retreated into suspicious silence, still searching for an angle. Why had Giovanni wanted to be set up with her? Was he doing penance for something? Not that she was a troll who only came out from under her bridge for vittles, but still. No one had ever been "dying" to be set up with her before. What had Giovanni seen in her that made him ask her out?

She had spent more time staring at her reflection since the conversation with Jess than she had at any other time during her previous twenty-six years, so long she was in danger of becoming like those birds that only need a mirror for companionship. And she always came back to the same conclusion: she was kind of meh. She would never describe herself as ugly, mostly because she had her mother's voice still ringing in her head, telling her she was beautiful no matter what the other kids said. But neither would she say she was a knockout. Her long and glossy hair was her best feature, and that was rather depressing. Lots of people had good hair. But horses and llamas had good hair, too. If she had to choose a standout feature, she would have picked a killer body or a drop-dead face. She would like to say that maybe it was her sparkling personality that had attracted Giovanni's attention, but that wasn't true, either. She was a high school librarian, and she lived up to the stereotype. Thoughtful, bookish, intelligent, she could spend the rest of her life in a cave with a good book and never emerge again.

The only thing different about her was that lately she had been working on a bucket list, a sort of farewell to her twenties. The list wasn't exciting, but maybe it had changed her in some subtle way. Maybe it had made her more interesting. Ironically, going on a blind date was one of the things on her list. So even when the date inevitably failed to work out, at least she would be able to cross something off her list. Hopefully that would be enough to keep her warm on cold nights and not torment her with what might have been.

"This is as good as it's going to get," she told her reflection and made a mental note to stop talking to herself before she turned into a weird old maid who talked to herself. She was wearing makeup, to the extent that she had even curled her eyelashes with a retro wand passed down from her grandmother. It was probably a strike against her that she took beauty tips from a woman who still believed a woman's best asset was her girdle.

Her dress wasn't new, but it was her lucky dress, the one that was not too dressy, not too casual. The strappy sandals were new, and they were killing her feet. Her hair wasn't up to par but, even with the humidity, looked passable. *And he said he wants to go out with you,* she encouraged her reflection. Whatever madness had overtaken him, he must have seen something in her he liked. So maybe she should stop staring at herself in critical appraisal and get on with it so she wasn't late.

They were meeting at the farmer's market to keep things casual. Jessamine has emphasized the word casual so much that Vivian's suspicion had increased to near cynicism. If Giovanni wanted things to be so casual and nonchalant, it was a wonder he had asked her out in the first place. Maybe he was one of those men who scared easily. Maybe she should wear a sandwich board that read, "Not Looking For Commitment." Lucky for him, in her case it would be true. While she wasn't opposed to finding love, she also wasn't desperately searching. She was an introvert's introvert: as happy on her own as she was with a small group of close friends. She had no need to "put herself out there" to find a man. If it happened, it happened. If not, well, that was what books and Netflix were for.

Still, even after all of her inspiring self-pep talks and all of the encouragingly pithy memes she had put on her Pinterest board, Vivian felt nervous. Her stomach was almost on the verge of revolt. She arrived at the Saturday morning farmer's market, their chosen meeting place, and white-knuckled the steering wheel, forcing a few deep breaths.

This is one morning of your life. If it doesn't work out, you'll return to your life as if nothing ever happened. Would she, though? That was her fear. Not that things wouldn't work out with Giovanni—that was a foregone conclusion. But what if the date made her yearn for things she didn't have, things that were out of her control? What if she suddenly became one of those women willing to do anything for a husband and child? Was it possible that one date with a gorgeous—at least in her opinion—man would mar the peaceful status quo of her life?

No, she wouldn't let it. She would be casual, as Jessamine said.

"I'm casual," she told herself. Then, "Shut up, stop talking to yourself, get out of the car before you die of heat stroke or someone sees you talking to yourself." She tucked her keys in her purse, checking twice to make sure she had them before she locked the door. Her purse was a tidy, perfectly portioned cross-body bag because she was more into function than fashion and the thought of paying an obscene amount of money for someplace to store her money set her teeth on edge. The bag was like everything in her life—tidy, well-organized, and pragmatic. She carried her phone, tinted lip balm, a compact with mirror and powder, her wallet, and keys. Today she had added a bit more makeup in case she needed to do a touchup and the extra weight made her feel off balance, as if she would be slanting slightly toward the right all day. She ignored the feeling and tried not to limp in her ill-fitting sandals as she went forward to meet Giovanni.

*G*iovanni felt warm. He wasn't sure if that was because he was wearing pants on a hot morning (what did one wear for a morning outdoor date? He should have asked Jessamine) or because he was more nervous than he was willing to admit. Having decided that he wanted to be set up, he had begun to think about his future. What if Vivian was the one? What if he was about to have a—casual—date with the mother of his children? His mind wandered as he pictured telling his future offspring the story. *Your mother and I had our first date at a farmer's market.*

The date venue had been Vivian's idea, and Giovanni liked it. He liked her for thinking of it. It was so much better than the standard dinner and a movie, and light years ahead of the "hanging out" his little brother, Moss, did. Giovanni was old fashioned, and he didn't like to "hang." He liked dates, real formal dates, like walking through a farmer's market with the possible mother of his children.

His eyes scanned the horizon as he tried not to fret. She was three minutes late, a point out of her favor. Giovanni didn't like tardiness. He appreciated punctuality, neatness, rules, and order. A place for everything, and everything in its place. Those were words to live by, in his opinion.

"Excuse me, hi."

His eyes stopped scanning the horizon and came to rest on the diminutive woman in front of him. He smiled at her, blinking in vague recognition. She looked familiar somehow, as if he should know her. But for the life of him he couldn't recall her.

"I'm Vivian," she said, the name sounding like a question, as if she sensed his confusion.

No you're not, he almost said, but stopped himself in time. Forcing a smile to his rubbery lips, he repeated the name as if he had never heard it before. "Vivian."

"Sorry I'm late," she rushed on. "I was standing there, waiting for you to approach, but you looked lost in thought, so I moved closer."

He was nodding like a bobblehead. What had happened? Where was his breathtaking, perfect goddess Vivian? The woman before him was nice looking, but in a cute sort of way, like a rose-lipped baby doll compared to the real-life Barbie he had been expecting. He pressed his hand to his stomach. "Can you excuse me for a minute? Just have to use the bathroom."

"It's there," she pointed behind him, a concerned expression on her face. He dodged into the restroom, whipped out his phone, and pounded a text to his sister.

Where is Vivian?

Jessamine replied:

She's there. She texted me two minutes ago.

Giovanni's thumbs moved so quickly auto correct was in high dudgeon.

No, Vivian has blond hair, blue dyes. Eyes. She's ball. Tall.

His sister's reply was equally as prompt and urgent.

THAT'S VIVICA, YOU DUMB CLUCK! I swear, Giovanni, you do anything to hurt Vivian, and I will rip your still-beating heart right out of your chest!

Giovanni felt the bottom drop from beneath him. He would have leaned on the wall, if the wall weren't covered in all manner of disgusting whatnots. He had asked for the wrong woman. Now he remembered meeting Vivian and Vivica together, the tall blond note of perfection and the equally forgettable sidekick. He had mixed up their names. *Stupid, stupid, stupid.* The worst part was that Jess would never set him up with Vivica now, not after this. And he was stuck for an entire morning with Vivian, a woman he hadn't given a thought to, a woman he knew less than nothing about. Unless…what if he wasn't stuck with her? She already thought he was sick. What if he used that excuse to cancel the date? Better yet, what if he could sneak away without her ever knowing?

He chanced a look out the door. She was looking away from the bathroom. He could slip away now and she would be none the wiser. He took a breath, preparing to make his escape when he thought of his sister. She would kill him, literally hunt him down and kill him dead if he ditched one of her friends, especially this one for whom she seemed to have a particular soft spot. He dithered in the doorway, right and wrong and fear of his sister waging battle inside him.

Vivian's phone chirped with a text from Jessamine. She pulled it out, not sure what to expect. At first the text made no sense.

***THAT'S VIVICA, YOU DUMB CLUCK!** I swear, Giovanni, you do anything to hurt Vivian, and I will rip your still-beating heart right out of your chest!*

Then it all came clear in an instant. Giovanni hadn't wanted her. He had wanted Vivica, like all men. On her own, Vivian had a chance, but next to her friend, she had become used to feeling invisible. It had never bothered her before, the fact that other men preferred Vivica's striking perfection to her own more subtle prettiness, but then the contrast had never been so stark before. Obviously Giovanni had asked to be set up with Vivica and gotten her instead. And, worse, Vivian had somehow been made aware of the fact by being accidentally copied into their private text. This explained his blank look of surprise when she showed up and his sudden dodge into the bathroom. Clearly he wasn't coming back out again.

No harm, no foul, she tried to tell herself, but the deep sting of rejection was there, and it hurt more than she wanted to admit.

Well, I'm not going to stand around here and wait like a loser, she said and began walking briskly away, staring blankly yet intently at the vendor stalls as if they were the most interesting thing she had ever seen.

"Care for a treat?" A man's voice startled her out of her self-pitying reverie. She was somehow standing in front of a vendor's stall being run out of an old van that looked like The Mystery Machine. Any minute she expected Scooby and the gang to pop their heads out and start talking about ghosts.

"Uh," Vivian said, forcing herself to look at what he was selling. There was a lot of granola and something made with hemp. The whole stand smelled like a gathering of *Grateful Dead* fans. "Sorry, I'm not a fan of granola," she said and started to move away.

"Wait, I have something special, something I only bring out for beautiful ladies." He turned to reach into the van. Vivian shouldn't trust him, she should walk away. But her self-esteem had taken such a beating in the last five minutes that his compliment, well-practiced and shallow as it may be, felt like a sweet balm to her battered spirit. She waited while he searched in his van and returned with a platter of brownies.

"These are special," he said.

Vivian didn't want the brownies. But no one else was buying from him, and he seemed so nice. She could buy one and dump it when he wasn't looking.

"How much for one?" she asked.

"Five for the whole platter," he said.

"That's a bargain," she said, smiling. His answering smile lit his face.

"You're going to like these, I guarantee it," he said.

She nodded as she reached in her purse and handed him a ten dollar bill. "Keep the change," she said.

He winked at her as he tucked the ten into his pocket and Vivian's smile felt more genuine. At least she had made an old guy feel good today, so the morning hadn't been a total waste. She turned toward her car and ran, almost literally, into Giovanni.

"Hey, you disappeared," he said. "Sorry I was in the bathroom for so long."

Her surprise at seeing him rendered her momentarily speechless. What was he doing there? Pity? No, they were strangers; pity wouldn't be enough to keep him there. Then she remembered the warning in Jessamine's text. Fear of his sister was all that kept him there at this point. She should do the nice thing and let him off the hook, but all of a sudden she didn't feel like being nice. She felt like having a good date with a handsome man and salvaging what was left of her morning. And her pride. She felt like showing him such a fun time that he regretted not asking her out in the first place. She felt like punching him in his stupid, handsome, Vivica-preferring face. So she held the platter of treats aloft.

"Brownie?"

He blinked warily at her sudden change in expression. "Sure, I love chocolate."

"Me, too," she said as they both took a bite of brownie.

"These are amazing," Giovanni said when he could talk.

He was right. They were possibly the best brownies Vivian had ever tasted. She couldn't quite place what was unique about them, but something she had never tasted in a brownie before.

"Where did you get them?" Giovanni asked.

"From…" Vivian turned to point to the old man with the weird van, but he was gone. "Strange."

"From Strange?" Giovanni asked sincerely.

He was looking around for a vendor marked, "Strange." Vivian had no idea why that struck her funny, but it did, and she laughed, a burble of pure enjoyment that made him smile.

"Giovanni, you want to get out of here?" she asked.

"What did you have in mind?" he asked.

"I know a place," she said and ate another bite of brownie.

CHAPTER 3

It started with the Roadhouse.

Vivian had never been there, of course, but she had heard the kids at school talk about it. It was a biker bar, known for loud music and good burgers. The password was a secret, one Vivian knew because she overheard her student assistant say it once. They drove her car, and Vivian led the way inside, Giovanni tagging cagily behind her as if he expected at any moment to either be attacked or have Vivian turn around and say, "Just kidding, let's get out of here."

But she didn't. Instead she stalked purposefully to the door and knocked. A pair of eyes appeared behind a hidden peephole.

"Password," the voice growled.

"Indian," Vivian said, having discerned previously that the word referred to a brand of motorcycle and not a politically incorrect description of Native Americans.

"Get in," the growly voice said, and the door opened as if by magic. Inside was an unimpressive plywood structure with a well-used bar and old-fashioned jukebox. Despite the early hour, the place was loaded with bikers. Vivian and Giovanni, in their respective dress and chinos, stood out like proverbial sore thumbs. But no one yelled at them and told them to go away, as Vivian secretly feared might happen. Instead a waitress yelled to sit down and she'd be with them, "as soon as I finish with these losers."

"You come here often?" Giovanni asked as he sat and began reading the menu posted on the back of a vinyl record.

"As often as I can get away from the library," she said. He nodded, and she took satisfaction in the fact that he wasn't sure if she was joking or not. "What about you? Do you have any special hangouts?"

"My mom's house," he said unashamedly. "I'm your typical Italian son—I love my Mama. And her meatballs and gravy."

"It must be interesting to be from such a large family," she said. It was just her and her sister. There were five Samperi children, each of them more boisterous than the last.

"If by interesting you mean loud, then yes."

"Do you miss Brooklyn?" Everyone knew that the family had moved from New York and, even though they had been in Kentucky for almost two decades, in the eyes of the town, they were still from New York.

"I don't remember much, but my oldest brother, Joe, makes the stories sound fun."

"Have you been to Italy?" she asked.

"Nah, but my parents dream of going someday. We'll make it happen, if we can ever get them to retire."

"That's my dream, to go and immerse myself in the culture, to pick up some of the language."

"*Sei piu bella di quanto mi sia reso conto,*" he rattled off in flowing Italian.

Vivian actually felt a swoon coming on, and she was a diehard non-swooner. There was something about a man who was fluent in another language that had that effect on her. "You speak Italian," she said dumbly.

"Some. My dad used it on us when he yelled, so I mostly know the angry words. What about you? Do you know any other languages?"

"I can read Old English, comes in handy when your undergrad is in literature."

"Say something," he said.

She spouted off a few lines of *Beowulf* in its original form. "Nice," he said, nodding appreciatively. "So you have your master's?" There was a tiny hint of his former Brooklyn accent. It blended effortlessly with the Kentucky drawl he'd acquired, making him sound sweet and a little bit exotic.

"I have my MLS, a master's in library science." She took pity on him and gave up the pretense that he knew anything about her. "I'm a high school librarian, your typical book nerd."

"I like to read, but in my job the only words I ever see are, 'Caution: May Cause Electrocution.'"

All of a sudden Vivian hated that he was funny. He was supposed to be dull; it would make him easier to forget when this was over. But he spoke Italian, liked to read, and had a self-deprecating sense of humor. *Danger, danger, danger.*

He glanced at his menu again. "What do you recommend?"

"Burgers," she said, though of course she had never had one.

"Sounds good, I'll have a burger and a sweet tea," he said to the waitress who was now standing beside them. Vivian loved that they were in a rowdy bar and he was secure enough to order tea.

"I'll have the same," she said.

The waitress smiled in a mocking sort of way. "Teetotalers have to do a song," she said, pointing to the small area of the bar that served as a karaoke stage.

"This is the strangest bar I've ever been to," Giovanni said. Turning to Vivian he added, "Do you sing every time you come, or do you secretly booze it up when I'm not here?"

"I love to sing," she evaded. It was too late to tell him she had never been to the cool secret bar, and had never sung karaoke anywhere ever. It was so far outside her comfort zone that it wasn't even on her bucket list.

"What do you think—whiskey or a song?" Giovanni asked.

Vivian stared at the makeshift stage. Could she really sing in front of this man and a bar full of raucous strangers? "Solo or duet?" she asked.

"Definitely duet," he said. He stood and pulled back her chair.

People in the bar began to hoot and holler as they stood by the microphone and made their selection.

"This one, I think," Giovanni said. Vivian agreed and "Islands in the Stream" began to play. At first they were timid, but when they realized people were stomping in encouragement and not derision, they got into it. By the end, Vivian had channeled her inner Dolly Parton.

"You can really sing," Giovanni said over the din of the hooting and clapping crowd.

"Show choir, baby," Vivian said and felt her cheeks warm. She had never called anyone "baby" before, least of all a date, but he merely smiled.

"That was fun," Giovanni said, sounding surprised. When they sat, their food had arrived. Though they had each eaten an entire brownie, Vivian felt famished, as if she had never seen food before. She bit into her burger with gusto and closed her eyes, taking a moment to savor.

"I'll give you this, Vivian, you know your food. First the best brownie ever, and now the best burger. What other secrets are you hiding?"

"Wouldn't you like to find out?" Vivian said and had to take a sip of water to cool her warm cheeks. What had gotten into her? She never flirted this way with anyone, and now she couldn't seem to help herself. The burger was gone in a few bites. She downed two glasses of tea, and there was no more reason to linger. Giovanni paid the check, despite her protests that they could split, but before they could leave, someone began to call for an encore.

"One more time?" Giovanni asked, indicating the karaoke stage.

"Bring it," Vivian said. This time they sang, "I've Got You, Babe," by Sonny and Cher. By the end everyone in the bar had joined in. It was the perfect end to the perfect date. Vivian could go home and relax, leaving the morning behind her with a happy sense of wellbeing. But when they stepped outside, fate intervened again.

"Hey, there are still brownies. Care for dessert?" Giovanni asked. He opened the door, took out the platter, and handed her a brownie.

"I really shouldn't," Vivian said, knowing she would devour the entire thing in three bites. They shared their brownies while leaning against her car.

"Beautiful day," Giovanni commented between bites.

"The best," Vivian agreed. "I think you appreciate them more when you know summer is winding down." Although her summer had already come to a close two weeks before when school started.

"It's almost our quiet season," Giovanni commented. "Construction workers usually hate the winter because it means work dries up, but for me it's a nice break. More time to read."

She felt the same about winter, as if everything was going to bed, allowing her time alone with her books.

The brownies were finished. Reluctantly, Vivian reached into her purse for her keys when the door of the roadhouse opened and a man stepped out.

"Hey, Samperi, nice vocals. I didn't know you had it in you."

"This stays between you and me, Tom." Giovanni nodded to the man's motorcycle. "Nice ride."

"Thanks. This is my wife, Patsy. Patsy, Giovanni is one of those knucklehead Samperi boys I'm always complaining about."

Patsy nodded, looking curiously at Giovanni before turning her attention to Vivian.

"Hey, we're heading an hour south to another roadhouse. You guys in?" Tom said.

Giovanni patted Vivian's car. "I don't think we brought the right equipment."

Tom tossed him a set of keys. "Take Patsy's bike, she can ride with me. Come on, Samperi, the next place has wings."

Vivian expected Giovanni to toss the keys back with a laugh. Instead he turned to Vivian with raised brows. "Well, I do like wings. What do you say, Vivian?"

Vivian had never ridden a motorcycle. She was wearing a dress. She had school on Monday. There were a million reasons she should say no. Instead she heard herself say, "I like my wings spicy, Giovanni. Think you can handle the heat?"

"Try me," he said, and helped her onto the bike. There were no extra helmets. Previous to this moment, Vivian would have said she would never, ever ride a motorcycle without a helmet. It was sheer stupidity to do so. And yet here she was, tucking her hair into a bun and using a pen from her purse to secure it.

"Hey, that's kind of sexy," Giovanni said.

"They make you learn how to do this when you become a librarian. It's part of the ceremony," she said. She wrapped up the remaining brownies and tucked them in the bag at the back of the motorcycle.

"Must be awkward for the male librarians," Giovanni said. Then he started the motorcycle, and they were on their way.

CHAPTER 4

$\mathcal{V}$ivian felt like she was flying. It wasn't just the motorcycle, although the way the engine vibrated through her body was its own sort of magic. It was everything.

After the roadhouse with wings, they went with Tom and Patsy an hour south to another roadhouse that had line dancing.

"I made fun of the kids who went line dancing in high school," Giovanni said.

"I wasn't cool enough to make fun of the kids who went line dancing in high school," Vivian said, and yet they line danced for an hour and a half.

After that they split with Tom and Patsy. "Bring the bike back tomorrow, I know you're good for it, the old people are turning in," was Tom's admonition when they headed for home.

"Home?" Giovanni said, but it sounded like a question.

"I heard about an all night diner not too far from here," Vivian said. In truth she had ducked into the bathroom and looked on her phone for anything still open nearby.

"I could go for an omelet," Giovanni said, then, "I've never eaten this much in my life. I have no idea why I'm so hungry."

They went to the all night diner and ordered pancakes and omelets to split. It was almost midnight. Vivian was usually in bed by ten; she couldn't cover a yawn.

"I should get you home," Giovanni said. Then they looked across the street and saw a dance club. "You wanna?" he asked, cocking his head in the direction of the club.

"You have to ask?" she said, stifling another yawn.

"Two coffees to go, and our check," he said, holding a finger aloft to signal the waitress. Refueled with coffee, they headed across the street. They started to line dance, but the song changed to a slow country song.

"Don't tell me you can slow dance, too," Giovanni said.

"Six years of ballroom dance lessons with my only male cousin. The teenage years were riddled with awkwardness," she said. "Can you dance?"

"Oh, I can dance, Vivian," he said and then proved it.

Until that moment, the day had been filled with casual platonic banter and a lot of laughter. But as they danced, a genuine zing of attraction began to buzz between them. Vivian felt the power of it, but she had no idea what to do with it or how to prolong it, so she remained quiet. Giovanni was quiet, too. He seemed taken aback, almost bewildered by the unexpected feelings now zapping between them.

The quiet stretched as they walked to the parking lot, unaware that they were now holding hands. "I guess we should go home," Giovanni said. "Although we're almost in Gatlinburg. Want to see the mountains?"

Vivian did. She wanted to do anything to keep the magic of this day alive. The night had turned cold. Vivian had only her thin sweater to keep her warm. Giovanni searched the back bag of the motorcycle and unearthed a jacket. He handed it to her.

"You take it," she protested.

"I insist," he said. He placed it around her shoulders and brushed the hair off her neck.

It's still here, she thought with a thrill of realization. The zing was still bouncing between them. And it had grown stronger when he touched her. His hand lingered at her neck, and then he kissed her. It was the best, most romantic kiss of Vivian's life. When it ended, she was trembling, and not from the cold now seeping through her.

Giovanni seemed equally shaken by the kiss. Wordlessly he took a step back, helped her onto the motorcycle, and they were off. Vivian had thought they would head home now, but she was wrong. When Giovanni turned out of the parking lot, he headed south.

They drove to the mountains. The road began to twist and warp beneath them. It was exhilarating and a little frightening, even though Giovanni handled the machine like a master. Until the kiss, Vivian had kept a polite distance between them, but now she wrapped her arms around him and closed her eyes, savoring the maleness of him as his scent mingled with the crisp night air. They drove for what felt like forever until he finally turned around. Eventually Vivian realized they were in the city of Gatlinburg; her parents had taken her there for vacations when she was a little girl. She was immersed in the scenery when all of a sudden her sandal flew off.

She tapped Giovanni's shoulder, and he pulled into a parking lot.

"My sandal," she said, pointing to her bare foot. He nodded and trotted back the road a ways, using his phone as a flashlight to search. Eventually he returned with her lost shoe. Chuckling, he pushed the windblown hair out of his face. "Look where we are, Cinderella."

It was a 24-hour wedding chapel. Vivian smiled. He knelt and slipped the sandal on her foot. Taking her hand, he nodded toward the chapel. "You wanna?"

She laughed. "Sure."

He stood. He still had hold of her hand. His glance fell to the chapel, then back to her. He licked his lips. "No, really, Vivian. You wanna?"

"Okay," she said, and she might have squeaked.

After that everything was a blur. Giovanni paid the fee, a mere fifty dollars. A sleepy looking man in a black robe said their vows while a soundtrack wedding march played in the background. Vivian carried a rented bouquet. At the end of it, Giovanni kissed her, and the man in the robe had to clear his throat to get their attention.

They were silent as they signed the marriage certificate. The man handed them a card for a local hotel. "Ten percent off honeymoon special." Vivian studied the card, her muddled brain unable to comprehend the word "honeymoon" as it applied to her.

From then on they both assumed a quiet sort of urgency, as if they had to finish what they started before they came to their senses. Giovanni's hand shook as he registered for the hotel, and Vivian's trembled as she used the bathroom to freshen up. She wouldn't look at herself in the mirror, not wanting to know what she might find in her reflection. If it was all a dream, she didn't want to know until tomorrow.

The next morning, Vivian woke first.

She had wondered if she would remember any of the previous night's events, and she had her answer as soon as her eyes opened. She remembered every moment in vivid detail. Every whisper, every caress, it was all there, stored in her permanent memory bank. She rolled over to study Giovanni, now lying beside her. He was still asleep. What would he think, what would he say? She wanted to reach out a finger and trace it along his bare chest, but her bravado from the previous day had disappeared. Now she felt only trepidation, and nausea caused by so much food.

His eyes fluttered. Vivian quickly lay back down and feigned sleep. He stirred and sat up. His phone beeped. He reached for it and began checking his messages. Neither of them had checked their phones since the morning before, a miracle in and of itself. Now as he began to scroll, reality came crashing back. Vivian could sense it in the hunch of his shoulders, could hear it in his muttered Italian. She had no idea what he was saying, but she knew it couldn't be good. She squeezed her eyes closed, waiting for the inevitable blow to drop, the "this is a mistake" talk.

He leaned closer and stroked a finger down her cheek. "Vivy."

He had started calling her that sometime in the night. Vivian liked it. No one had ever used a nickname on her before. She had always been plain Vivian.

"Mmm," she said, her stomach a knotted ball of nerves.

"I think we need to talk." Reluctantly she opened her eyes and he continued. "I need you to know I've never done anything like this before. I'm Mr. Predictable. I don't do rash or impulsive, and I guess things like this are why."

She sat up, unable to bear to hear him go on. The best defense was a good offense, right? "It was all my fault."

He smiled indulgently. "How was this your fault?"

"The brownies."

"How did brownies have anything to do with this?"

"Because I think they were laced with pot."

He stared at her, unblinking. "What?"

She told him about the weird guy in the van. "I didn't give it much thought before, but last night it hit me. I mean, we were acting so strange, so unlike ourselves. What else could it have been?"

He put his head in his hands. "I took pot? I've never done drugs before. This is not good, on top of everything else."

"I'm sorry," she said. She was near tears, and she hated that. Above all she didn't want to lose control in front if him.

"It's not your fault. Brownies, no brownies, we both lost our heads. We'll get an annulment. Come on, I'll take you home." He stood, still looking at her. "I, uh, I'll need my shirt."

He had put it on her last night, the last thing before they went to sleep. "Could you hand me my dress and…things?" she asked. Her voice sounded the way it did when she was trying not to cry. Thankfully he didn't know her well enough to realize.

He handed her the dress, bra, and underwear delicately, as if they were made of gossamer, then turned away while she changed. She studied his shoulder blades for a second. Last night her finger had traced over them as if they were a part of her. Today they were off limits.

Quickly, she shrugged out of his shirt and into her own clothes.

"Giovanni, don't worry about taking me home. My friend from college lives here, and I'm due for a visit with her."

"Are you sure?" he asked, but his relief was palpable.

"I'm positive."

"I feel like I'm dumping you in the middle of nowhere," he said.

"I know this area like the back of my hand, and I'm only a few hours from home. Please, go, return your friend's motorcycle before he puts out an APB on us." She smiled.

His lips turned up tentatively in return. "All right. I'll call you later. And I'll get a lawyer to take care of, you know." His hand waved in her direction.

"Sure, sure," Vivian said. Her lips were stretched so tight they might pop like an overstuffed piñata.

"Do you want me to grab you a coffee from downstairs or anything before I go?"

"No, I'll be fine. I might grab a shower before I call my friend. I can't imagine seeing anyone looking like this." *Except the stranger I married and spent the night with, that is.*

"If you're sure," he said, edging toward the door.

"I'm positive, you're fine. Have a safe trip back."

"Thanks, you too." His back bumped the door. He paused, not sure how best to finally extract himself from the situation. She could almost read the uncertain thoughts flitting across his features. Should he kiss her? Hug? Shake hands? What?

"Bye," she said, tossing him a little wave to go with the unwavering smile.

"Bye," he said. He eased out the door, but it still closed with a bang behind him. Vivian waited a few beats to make sure he was really gone, and then she checked her watch. Checkout was at eleven. It was a quarter to.

Quickly, she hopped in the shower, scrubbed herself from head to toe, and dried her hair as best she could in the few minutes she had. She packed her purse and headed downstairs, grabbing a cup of coffee on her way by the front desk. Once outside, she pulled out her phone and checked the battery; it was almost dead. There was enough juice to make one call, and it was the call she least wanted to make. So she texted instead.

Can you come get me? I'm at the coffee shop in Gatlinburg.

Her sister replied immediately.

WHAT? Why are you in Gatlinburg?

Vivian sat on the curb outside the hotel and thought how best to reply. What to say to her sister? I ate some pot brownies and married a stranger? I got jilted on my honeymoon? I had the best night of my life and now it's over forever? I married the man of my dreams and am having it annulled poste haste?

Long story. Can you come?

It'll take hours, her sister replied.

I know, thanks. Vivian finished her text and started to walk. First she explored every store she could find, on both sides of the street. When she grew tired, she bought a book, a bagel, and a coffee, and retired to the coffee shop to wait for her sister. If only her college friend weren't away for the summer she could have called her, as she had told Giovanni she would. They could have had a nice visit. Her friend wouldn't have asked any intrusive questions that required awkward answers. Her older sister was another matter entirely. She would only allow so much evasion. But Vivian wasn't ready to talk about the events of the past twenty four hours. In fact, she might never talk about them. They might go to her grave as what they were —a crazy, forgotten weekend, the last hurrah of a twenty-something female.

The more she thought about not telling anyone about what had happened between her and Giovanni, the more she liked the idea. After all, it was no one's business, no one but hers and Giovanni's. Absolutely no one had to know how impulsively she had acted. And no one would ever have to learn how horribly she had been rejected, not once but twice. First by not being the right date and then by being the wrong wife at the wrong time. She couldn't shake the dreadful feeling that if it had been Vivica who rashly married Giovanni, he wouldn't have rushed out to get an annulment first thing.

By the time her sister, Annie, arrived, Vivian had pushed her hasty nuptials to a place so deep inside not even she was sure they'd happened. She would tell no one, ever. And she was certain Giovanni would do the same thing. They would get a quickie annulment, and no one would ever know what they'd done. And as for all the newfound feelings and desires now burgeoning inside her, well, they'd have to die eventually, wouldn't they? For her sake, she certainly hoped so.

CHAPTER 5

Giovanni had eaten the same thing for breakfast since he moved out of his mother's house—a bowl of bran with a cup of coffee and half a banana. Every morning, the same thing with no variation. He wore the same assortment of clothes every day —khaki pants with a black or gray polo shirt. For special occasions he wore either a blue or white button down shirt. He had worn the same style of tortoiseshell glasses since he was fifteen years old. When his Toyota Camry went toes up, he replaced it with another Toyota Camry in the same color. He was a predictable person who took comfort in routine, the more predictable, the better. That was why he couldn't fathom how he now found himself married to a stranger. What had possessed him? And it was as if he had been possessed, as if a free spirit had taken over his body and led him down a path of unrighteousness.

The worst part was the guilt. Not for his own behavior, but for taking Vivian along with him. She was innocent. Well, not so innocent, he thought as he remembered a few choice scenes from their brief honeymoon. No, no, no, he shouldn't think of her that way. His wry smile slipped back into a frown. How was he going to undo the mess he had made with the least amount of collateral damage?

"I notice you skipped out on family dinner yesterday." Jessamine spoke from very nearby. Giovanni had been expecting her all day, especially since he had ignored all twelve of her texts. Did she know? Had Vivian told her by now? Women talked about stuff like that, didn't they?

"I had stuff to do," Giovanni said.

"Ma was upset," his sister said.

"Ma's always upset if one of us misses a meal." Sunday family dinners had been a part of his life for as long as he could remember. His mother would accept few valid excuses to miss one.

"So, the date," Jessamine began. Sweat exploded through the pores on Giovanni's forehead. "How was it?"

Was she testing him? He shrugged.

"Come on, Giovanni, I heard from Vivian. I want to hear your take."

"What did she say?" he asked and had to clear his parched throat.

Jessamine pulled out her phone and read. "Thanks for the fix up. Not a love match, but it was fun."

Giovanni let out a breath he didn't know he'd been holding. She didn't know. And if she didn't know then no one in his family knew. They were like a beehive that way—information was communicated to the group simultaneously.

"It was like she said. We had fun." *Boy, did we,* he thought and had to suppress another inappropriately-timed smile.

"Are you going to call her again?" Jessamine asked.

"I'm sure I'll talk to her again at some point," Giovanni replied.

His sister expelled a puff of air that seemed to say, *Men are pigs.* For once he was inclined to agree with her. "I suppose you want me to set you up with Vivica now." She was spoiling for a fight, but then she usually was. Jessamine had been born with a chip on her shoulder so large it was amazing she had fit through the birth canal.

"I'll think about it,"

In trying to head off any fires, he had still somehow said the wrong thing. She pinned him with a frown. "What's with the sudden change of heart? Last week you were dying to go out with her."

"Well, Saturday's date showed me that maybe I'm not as ready to date as I thought I was," he said.

Jess grinned. "I should have known. Mr. Boring takes one step out of the ordinary and has to retreat all the way back to home base."

"Yep, that's me, Mr. Predictable," he agreed, but the irony was lost on his sister. Or maybe it wasn't. She paused mid-step, her head cocked to the side as she studied him.

"You're weird today, little brother."

"I think my bran was past its expiration date," he said. She laughed, mussed his hair, and moved along.

Giovanni gave up the pretense of wiring whatever he was supposed to be wiring. He sat and stared at the half-finished wall in front of him. He needed to clear his head. He needed to focus. He needed to end his ill-considered marriage before anyone found out about it. But as he sat, his thoughts morphed from the end of his marriage to the beginning as he replayed the day in his head. And somehow all thoughts of calling a lawyer slipped quietly away.

⚷

*V*ivian was having a much worse time of things. First there was her sister who wouldn't take Vivian's cryptic silence for an answer.

"Were you visiting Adele?"

"Adele is away for the summer," Vivian replied, her gaze focused vaguely out the window.

"Did you know that when you went to Gatlinburg?"

"Yes."

"Who did you go with?"

"A friend."

"Which friend?"

"Someone you don't know."

"Vivian!" Annie snapped. "What is going on?"

"Nothing, Annie. I went to Gatlinburg with a friend, but my ride back got all mixed up. End of story."

"And it has nothing to do with why you're sitting here like a zombie."

"I'm tired," Vivian said. "I didn't get much sleep last night."

"What were you doing?"

Vivian laughed and covered her mouth, shaking her head.

"What does that mean?" Annie asked. She was becoming irritated. First she'd had to give up her entire Sunday to retrieve her little sister from some sort of road trip gone wrong, and now Vivian wouldn't say a word about it. It was too much.

"I had plans today, you know," Annie added.

"I know, and I'm really sorry. But I couldn't...I couldn't get back the same way I came."

"What does that mean?" Annie asked.

"Annie, I don't want to talk about it, please." Vivian rested her head against the window and didn't say another word. Her sister darted worried glances at her the rest of the way home. She stopped asking until they arrived at the roadhouse where she'd left her car.

"What is this place?"

"They have good burgers," Vivian said.

"Why was your car here overnight?"

"Because I left it here."

"Vivian!"

"Annie, someday maybe I can tell you the whole story, but right now I'm tired and hungry and sore and I want to go home and go to bed."

"Why are you sore?" Annie asked, but Vivian shook her head and refused to answer. "I'm going to tell Mom," Annie threatened.

"Please don't," Vivian said quietly and her eyes looked so sad and so pleading that Annie's anger dissolved.

"Hey, you can talk to me, all right? I'll keep your secret, whatever it is."

Vivian nodded. "If I decide to talk about it, you'll be the first to know," she said. She gave her sister a hug, climbed wearily into her car, and drove home.

Now it was Monday and though Vivian had been delighted to

return to work and her routine, nothing felt the same. It was as if the weekend had left an indelible imprint on her; body, mind, and soul. But that was ridiculous, wasn't it? People had one-night stands all the time and somehow survived. Did they feel this way? Technically she had married the guy, so she wasn't sure it was the same. But it was, wasn't it? They'd had one night together and she hadn't heard from him since. She felt unclean and weary, so very weary. What had once been a simple life now seemed muddled.

"Hey, Miss Haslett, you have a minute?" One of the male teachers stuck his head in the door.

"Sure, Mr. Kincaid, what do you need?" It had been odd to Vivian to call coworkers by their last names, but only at first. Now it had become such second nature she barely gave it a thought.

"I was wondering if that book I asked you to order had come in yet."

"Not yet, but I'm expecting a delivery this afternoon. I'll let you know."

"You do that," he said, and then he winked at her.

Vivian smiled weakly as he walked away. What had that been about? Had the wink seemed conspiratorial, or was it her? Did he somehow know about her weekend? No, she was being paranoid. But what else could it have been about? He was married, wasn't he? No. According to the gossip mill, he was in the midst of a divorce.

On the prowl, Vivian thought with distaste. Then with no small amount of sadness she realized she would also soon be out a marriage. *Well, Vivian, could your life get any more messed up?* The answer, of course, was a resounding yes.

CHAPTER 6

Two weeks after the hasty nuptials, a tree fell through Vivian's bedroom. At five in the morning she heard a crack, followed by a boom, and then wind and rain were blowing on her face. She bolted upright and nearly smacked her cheek on a branch.

"Oh," she said to no one in particular. "Oh, my. What the world?" She reached for her light, but the power was out. She froze, trying to calculate the location of her outside power lines. Were any downed lines on her house? Was she in danger? Could she be electrocuted? Would her house burn down?

She turned her phone on and held it aloft, using its weak light to try and illuminate the piece of Mother Nature now decorating her living space. There were no lines tangled in the branches, and there was no arcing sound of live wires. Still, she hopped far away from the bed and landed on both feet, something she read to do in case her car ever collided with an electric pole. Holding her arms out straight like a gymnast sticking a landing, she regained her balance and tried to think. What was the first thing to do in this situation? *Restore power.* She looked up her electric company and made the call. It went to an automated teller, of course, because who would answer the phone at five in the morning?

Next she called her insurance company and left a message. After that she had no idea what to do. Her dad might know what to do, but her parents had moved away from their children when they retired. She hated to bother him so early in the morning when there was nothing he could do. There was her brother-in-law, but Annie's husband wasn't what one would call "handy." Plus Annie would kill her if she woke the kids so early in the morning.

Outside, the rain was coming to an end. The day was supposed to be sunny, one thing in Vivian's favor. At least her carpet and furniture wouldn't be ruined by a deluge.

Tarps, she thought. She would need some to cover everything until repairs could be made. But where did one buy tarps? And how would she put them on her roof? That wasn't such a problem; now that her roof had become a part of her bedroom, she could probably stand on a chair and shove a tarp through.

Her mind was muddled. She reached for the coffee pot before remembering the power was out. How was she supposed to get ready with no electricity? Her house was on a pump system—without power she had no water. She would have to go to Annie's to get ready. She tamped down a feeling of dread. Annie had stopped trying to probe her over the mystery weekend in Gatlinburg. But her eyes followed Vivian with no small amount of suspicion and a hint of pity, as if Vivian had been jilted. What was most bothersome about that was that she had, in fact, been jilted.

Her thoughts drifted to her finances and her dread almost turned to panic. Why had she bought a house? At the time, it had seemed like the sensible thing to do. But she had vastly underestimated the many hidden costs of owning a home. With so much college debt, she was barely keeping her head above water. Even with insurance to help, she was sure to have a massive deductible to cover the elephant-size hole now in her bedroom. She had so little in savings. What was she going to do? She had to make her mind stop thinking of things.

With a solid hour left to kill until she could reasonably go to her sister's, she grabbed a flashlight and a book and curled up on the couch with a blanket. She read the same words five times before giving up. Since *the event*—her mind refused to call it a marriage—reading, her lifelong best friend, had betrayed her. She couldn't engage in anything. Even the book she had been so interested in before sat gathering dust on her bedside. She wouldn't allow herself to analyze this. Instead she had turned to binge watching television. Except she couldn't afford cable, so she found herself watching a whole lot of PBS. She and Curious George were now on a first name basis, and she had spent so much time watching The Man in the Yellow Hat that she was beginning to view him as a romantic lead. Although her newfound interest in him did not come without questions. He had a two-bedroom apartment in Manhattan, a home in the country, and a convertible, yet he never went to work. Trust fund? What exactly was his association with the museum? Artifact smuggling? And why yellow?

The book tumbled from her hand and she realized she was staring at the blank television once again puzzling over Curious George's mysterious roommate. *Is it any wonder Giovanni didn't want you? You're so weird,* she thought and quickly changed the mental dial. Any thoughts of Giovanni were strictly verboten. They hurt too much; the rejection was still too fresh, too raw. Instead she went back upstairs and gathered everything she would need to get ready. She drove through *McDonald's* for coffee and a McMuffin and ate in her car, watching the sunrise. If not so pathetic and lonely, it would have been a lovely start to the morning.

I was never lonely before, she thought with no small amount of bitterness. The bursts of bitterness were also new and unwelcome. *Before* she hadn't felt unwanted or second rate. *Before* she hadn't realized how singular and uninteresting her life was. Now all her deficiencies were in full view. Her life was small. Somehow that had always been okay, but that was *before.* Now she'd had a taste of adventure. Now she knew what it felt like to be desired by a man, if only for a brief glimmer. Everything after that one wild weekend felt like second best. *My life is a whole bunch of leftovers,* she thought as unbidden tears sprang to her eyes. She swiped impatiently at them. *No.* She hadn't cried and she wouldn't, not today. The real reason she was crying was because she had been awakened early by a tree falling through her roof. Her insurance rates would probably skyrocket, not to mention the hassle and money of getting everything fixed. Her budget was already stressed to the max. This was going to hurt. A lot. That was worth crying over, but not the other thing.

When she showed up on her sister's doorstep a little past dawn, her sister blinked sleepily at her and blurted, "You're pregnant."

"What? No, why would you even…no. I need to use your shower."

"What happened to your shower?" Annie asked, the suspicion in her tone the same as if Vivian had just asked for ten thousand dollars in small, unmarked bills.

"A tree fell through my house and knocked out the power."

"What? Are you all right? Come in." Finally, her sister moved aside and made her feel welcome.

"I'm fine, but I need to get ready for school. Can I use your shower?"

"Of course, of course. The kids aren't up yet. I'd suggest you hurry because the baby figured out how to open the door, even when it's locked. If you want privacy, I'd scoot."

Vivian didn't need to be told twice. Not only did she need to get ready for work before her nephew jimmied the lock, it was also a handy way to escape her sister's unwavering speculation. Annie had been watching her like she might be a secret drug mule since the weekend she picked her up in Gatlinburg. She showered in record time and was just drying her hair when her nephew propped open the door, giggling like every two year old who has just gotten away with something he knows he shouldn't.

Annie insisted she sit at the kitchen table and have a (second) cup of coffee. Her four-year-old niece, Gertrude, a mini-me of her mother, sat surveying her with a matching look of concern.

"So, how are you doing?" Annie asked in the same tone that people reserve for a widow, post-funeral. She might as well have chucked her under the chin and murmured, "How you holding up, slugger?"

"I'm a little harried this morning," Vivian said, taking a pointed glance at the clock. She had three minutes. Surely she could survive her older sister's speculation for three minutes.

"Are you ready to talk?" Annie asked.

"About what?" Vivian hedged.

"Vivian, come on. I know something happened that weekend." Beside her, Gertrude nodded in solemn agreement. Vivian wondered if Annie and Gertrude had conversations about her. *Turn off* Bubble Guppies, *Gert. It's time to have a serious discussion about Aunt Vivian's life.*

Vivian gulped her coffee and regretted it immediately. It was lava hot, the way Annie liked it. She stood and spluttered a mouthful into the sink before turning on the tap and letting the cool water gush over her tongue.

"Aunt Vivian is drinking from the faucet," Gertrude tattled.

"Aunt Vivian's not herself lately," Annie said. Gertrude nodded as if it wasn't the first time she'd heard the words.

Burning her tongue, and trying to cool it, had taken Vivian's entire three minutes, so that she had time enough only to give Annie a side hug, pat her niece on the head, and jet out the door. Arriving at work should have been a blessed relief, but it wasn't. Mr. Kincaid sat in her office, a smile on his face and a cup of coffee in his hand. He stood as soon as she opened the door, handing her the cup of coffee.

"I brought you some teacher juice," he said.

"Oh, thank you," Vivian said, trying hard to force the proper mix of thankfulness and disinterest into her voice. For the last few weeks, he had been seeking her out. She hadn't been encouraging him, but neither had she told him to buzz off. The problem being that she wasn't sure he was actually interested in her. She didn't think of herself as the type of woman men turned to while going through a breakup. Unless it was in the platonic sense. She had always had lots of male friends, often preferring to be around men for their lack of drama. Never had any of those friendships ever turned to romance. So it was hard for her to determine if Mr. Kincaid was singling her out because he was lonely and in need of a friend or if he was hoping to make her his post-marriage rebound. Even without the complication of *the event*, she wouldn't have been interested in him. She didn't date married—or soon to be unmarried—men.

"What's wrong?" Mr. Kincaid asked with a bit more proprietary interest than Vivian found comfortable.

She waved her hand dismissively. "It's nothing. A minor house emergency."

"What's up?" he asked.

"A tree fell on my bedroom," she said. He had been mid-sip of coffee and he sputtered, almost spewing her with mocha-colored liquid. She grabbed a tissue from her desk, stuffed it into his hand, and watched while he used it to sop himself.

"Are you okay? You could have died," he said.

"It was no big deal, just a gaping hole and lack of electricity. I put a call in to my insurance company, and I'm sure they'll get it sorted out soon."

He stared at her, a dubious expression on his face that made her doubt herself. Was the hole a bigger deal than she realized?

"I'm going to get some tarps," she added lamely.

"I'll come with you," he said in that decidedly male way that made her feel both grateful and irritated. Irritated because he assumed she had no idea what she was doing. Grateful because she had no idea what she was doing.

"You don't need to, really, I'll be fine."

"It's no big deal. We'll go right after work. Maybe we could grab some supper when we're finished."

"Uh…" the word lingered as if her vocal cords were stuck on repeat. He didn't seem to notice.

"Good. I'll swing by for you later. Have a good day, and enjoy the coffee."

"Uh…" the single note continued to emerge from her throat. Had they made a date? Surely not. She would know if she was going on a date with a man, wouldn't she? She pushed it from her mind, determined to deal with it when the time came, but somehow the time never came. And that was how she found herself riding with him to the home improvement store after work. She still wasn't sure how she had let herself be talked into that. Now not only was she going on an errand and then out to dinner with him, she was stuck in the same car, unable even to leave when she wanted. The old her would never have let this happen. Everything was off since *the event.*

"Really, Mr. Kincaid," she sputtered, trying again to absolve herself even as she buckled the seatbelt in his car.

"Call me Evan, Vivian," he said.

"Evan, this is totally unnecessary. I can pick up tarps. I can drive."

"Meh," he said, waving her words away. Perhaps it wasn't that she wasn't saying the proper things to him, rather he was ignoring her protestations. The car began to move and she resigned herself to fate. She was going to the store with this man and then probably to dinner, but it wasn't a date. She would be clear on that point, especially with the smell of his wife's perfume still lingering in the car.

They arrived at the home improvement store and her mind turned to business. Tarps. The sooner she bought them, the sooner they could go. Mr. Kincaid, as she stubbornly still thought of him, was on leisure time, however. He meandered through the fasteners section and then lumber before finally making his way to the tarps.

"They're with the paint, Vivian," he said knowingly, steering Vivian in that direction. He was walking in front of her, like a shepherd, so that she had to step around him when they arrived at their destination. And that was when she saw them, Jessamine and Giovanni, standing together in the paint aisle, staring curiously at her.

CHAPTER 7

Jessamine's face broke into a smile of welcome as her eyes bounced from Vivian to Mr. Kincaid and back again.

"Vivian, hi," she said. Beside her, Giovanni bore a stoic expression, but his eyes also traveled between Vivian and her companion. Vivian felt her cheeks burning with a shame she in no way understood. Was it cheating on your husband if he wasn't really your husband and the man you were with wasn't really your date? Of course not. So why did she feel in such a mad rush to explain?

"A tree fell on my house," she blurted. Then, "Hi." For all intents and purposes she was speaking to Jessamine, but her mind was tuned on Giovanni. His eyebrows rose infinitesimally.

"Are you okay?" Jessamine asked.

Evan chuckled slightly. "That's what I said. Vivian's so casual about everything, it's hard to tell sometimes."

Vivian tamped down a burst of annoyance at his statement. He barely knew her. How was he already making generalizations?

"Vivian is level headed," Jessamine agreed.

I will not look at Giovanni, Vivian promised herself. She didn't want to see his assessment of her level-headedness.

Giovanni finally spoke. "How's your house?"

"Not great," Vivian admitted, her eyes finally creeping to his face as she fought a flush she prayed he couldn't see. A tendril of her hair picked that inconvenient moment to tumble onto her face. Relieved to have something to do, she put a hand up and pushed it back.

"What's the damage?" he asked. Did his gaze fall to her lips before bouncing back to her eyes? No, of course not. Must be wishful thinking on her part.

"I'm not sure, exactly, but there's a tree in my bedroom, so I'm going to say it's not good. And as of five this morning, I had no power."

"Ah, Vivian, that's the worst," Jessamine said. "Do you need anything?"

"Tarps," Vivian said and hoped her voice didn't squeak. She hadn't seen Giovanni since *the event*. And she had to run into him at Home Depot with an audience. Her face must be flaming. She only hoped she didn't break into a flop sweat and have a complete antiperspirant failure. Did Home Depot sell deodorant? She might need to find out.

"Are you headed home now? We could swing by and look at it," Jessamine volunteered.

"Oh, that's so sweet of you, but I'm sure you guys have other things to do," Vivian said.

"Plus I'm going to help her," Evan piped up.

"Are you in construction?" Giovanni asked.

"Only if you count constructing young minds," Evan said. Vivian fought a burble of nervous laughter at Giovanni's uncomprehending expression.

"Evan's a teacher at my school," Vivian said. "And Jessamine and her family are in the construction business," she told Evan, an understatement if there was one. They were the premiere builders and renovation experts in the tri-state area. Asking them to take a look at her paltry house would be like asking a famous heart surgeon to apply a bandage to a scratched finger.

"It's no trouble," Jessamine insisted.

"We could at least tell you if it's safe," Giovanni added, and Vivian lost the will to argue. Did it almost maybe sound like he cared about her safety?

The group stood around while Vivian bought tarps, and then headed for her home.

"I guess supper is going to be delayed a while," Evan said and it was hard to ignore the slight pout in his tone.

"Sorry," Vivian said absently, although she wasn't. She didn't want to go to supper with him.

"How do you know these people?" Evan asked.

"Jessamine and I became friends through a book club. Giovanni is her brother." *And my husband, in the most technical sense.*

"I could guess that. They look alike," Evan said with a hint of the reverential tone people used whenever they talked about Jessamine or Vivica. Vivian was the plain filling between an astoundingly beautiful friend sandwich. How had she attracted two such lovely friends who were so extreme in their looks? Vivica was cool and blond while Jessamine was all big black hair and stunning hazel eyes. On its own, her nose tended to look a little large and slightly hawkish, but in combination with the rest of her face and hair, she was arresting. And then there was Vivian, plain, vanilla Vivian, half a foot shorter than her friends, curvy, and with no distinguishing features save a full head of thick, glossy hair.

"Don't sigh, Vivian, we'll get your house straightened out," Evan said.

Vivian offered him a weak smile. She hadn't been thinking about her house, but his words made her feel guilty. He was being incredibly nice to her by taking her to the store and helping her with her house situation. She didn't want to be rude to him, but neither did she want to lead him on. How best to extricate herself from this sticky situation?

"Evan, I'm a little out of the loop at school, but it seems like I heard you and your wife had separated. Are you doing okay?"

He blinked a couple of times and for a minute she thought he might cry. At last he shrugged one shoulder. "It is what it is, you know? Sometimes things don't work out, even when you want them to."

She nodded, although she had no idea. If two people wanted to make something work, why couldn't it? But maybe his wife didn't want things to work. Maybe he was being rejected. That Vivian understood all too well.

"I'm sorry," she said. "Relationships can be really hard."

"Are you in one?" he asked.

"This is my house," she said, pointing unnecessarily to the only house on the block with a giant tree on it. Now that she could better see the damage in the light of day, she shuddered. The tree was quite large, and it had fallen on a good portion of her house. It was a wonder she hadn't been crushed in her sleep.

"Vivian, you could have died," Evan exclaimed as he parked and got out of the car.

"Oh, Vivian," Jessamine said, coming up along side her and placing an arm around her shoulders. Giovanni said nothing as he began making a slow circle of the house, his gaze sweeping expertly up and down.

"Let's go inside," Jessamine suggested when Vivian remained staring mutely at what had previously been a magnificent shade tree.

Vivian unlocked the door and noted immediately that the power was still out. At least her house was clean and she needn't be embarrassed over any untidiness as she led them through the living room and up the stairs.

Her bedroom felt hot and damp. She hugged the tarps to her chest like a security blanket. Had she bought enough? The hole looked larger than she remembered.

Beside her, Evan whistled appreciatively. "That is one gigantic tree." Jessamine strode fearlessly close to the tree and examined the hole.

"Yikes," Jessamine muttered.

"It's bad, huh?" Vivian said. She'd hoped that it was a small hole that could be easily patched, hopefully by the weekend, and then her life could resume uninterrupted.

"It's bad," Giovanni spoke from the doorway and Vivian turned to watch him. "There's a significant amount of structural damage. Part of the roof and some beams might need to be replaced. And a fair amount of rewiring will need to be done. I turned off the main breaker downstairs, along with your water. You won't be able to stay here."

"Oh," Vivian said. Evan reached out and gave her shoulder a comforting squeeze. Giovanni cleared his throat.

"I'm going to talk to Joe," Jessamine said to her brother.

Giovanni nodded. "We should be able to work it in," he said.

"Who's Joe?" Evan asked.

"Our brother," Jessamine supplied.

"How many of you are there?" Evan asked.

"Five," Jessamine said absently as she pulled out her phone and began to text.

"You guys are so busy, and you have such big jobs. I can get someone else to handle this," Vivian said, gesturing feebly to the tree and gaping hole that now represented her living space.

"It's going to be tricky," Giovanni said. "You don't want just anyone to handle a repair like this." It was hard not to focus on his accent, a hint of Brooklyn mixed with a trifle of Kentucky twang. But focusing on his accent was better than focusing on his beautiful face or any other intrusive memory of *the event*.

"Still, I feel awful to intrude on your schedule like this," Vivian protested. Jessamine was always talking about how busy they were, about how jobs piled up around them like three-day-old fish, about how every job seemed to be an emergency. Of course when Jessamine said it, she wasn't complaining. She was the sort of person who thrived on stress and deadlines.

"You need to learn to let people take care of you," Evan said with another hand to the shoulder.

Giovanni took a step closer. "You should pack. I don't like the look of that roof beam."

"He's right," Jessamine said as her thumbs blurred over her phone in a blinding series of texts. "Joe said we're good for tomorrow. Do you have a place to stay, Vivian? You're welcome to stay with me."

"Jessamine, I cannot even begin to tell you how much I appreciate all you're doing for me, thank you. And I do have somewhere to stay." She was still holding the tarps. She turned awkwardly to the tree, wondering what exactly to do with them. Should she shimmy through the hole in the roof and staple them up? It had seemed like such a simple thing—buy tarps, cover hole. Now there were more questions than answers. Should she put the tarps on the inside or the outside? And did she have a stapler that would work on her roof?

"I'll put the tarps up," Evan said.

"I can do it," Giovanni volunteered. "Since we're officially on the job, and all." He smiled. Vivian felt a little weak in the knees, but maybe it was a reaction to house stress and not a reaction to his beautiful face. "Do you have a ladder?"

"In the garage. The opener is on the wall."

"We were just heading out for a bite," Evan said, sounding a bit impatient.

"This might take a while," Giovanni said. He reached out and took the tarps from Vivian, his fingers accidentally brushing lightly over her stomach, which clenched at his touch.

"You should go," she was talking to Evan but looking at Giovanni. He froze. She tilted her head around him to put Evan in her sights. "I think I should stay while he's on the roof, I would feel better if I did. I'll walk you down."

"What about your car?" Evan said.

"I can walk to get it. The school is only a few blocks from here."

"It's two miles," Evan said, as if he had clocked it.

"I could use the exercise," Vivian said. At this point she felt almost desperate for him to go.

"I can take her to get it," Jessamine volunteered.

Vivian steered Evan to the door before he could find another reason to protest. "Thank you so much, Evan."

"I didn't do anything," he said, and the pout was back.

"You did, you were a real friend and sounding board. You took a heap of my stress and helped me buy the tarps."

Slightly mollified, he followed her silently to his car. "We didn't get to have dinner."

"I know, and I'm so sorry for the delay in food. You must be starved."

He shrugged, and then the smile reappeared. "Rain check, I guess. See you tomorrow, Vivian. Good luck with the hole." He was gone before she could reply.

Back upstairs, Jessamine was taking measurements and writing them on a piece of paper. Vivian got out a suitcase and began packing. "Are you seeing that guy?" Jessamine asked. She was one of those people who could successfully multitask, talking and taking complex measurements, for example.

"No, he's some guy from work. He's in the midst of a marital breakup."

"Uh-oh."

"Exactly. It's the weirdest thing, Jess. I've never been that girl who guys like."

Jessamine made a disgruntled noise.

"I'm not being self-pitying, I'm being honest. But Evan won't seem to take the hints that I'm not interested. And I've never had to do more than hint to get a guy to leave me alone before. I'm a bit baffled about what to do with him."

"Vivian, you don't see yourself clearly. You are adorable. More than that, you're warm and sweet."

"Those are exactly the traits men list when filling out an application for what they want in a puppy," Vivian said.

Jessamine rolled her eyes. "You are a treasure."

"I'm no Vivica," Vivian couldn't stop herself from saying.

Jessamine sighed and sank to the bed. "So you found out about that, did you? I was hoping I didn't actually copy you in that stupid text. I'm so, so sorry, Vivian."

Vivian smiled. "It's really okay. I know what Vivica looks like; I know how men see her."

"It's strange that you can see how men see her and not how they see you," Jessamine said.

"I'm a realist. I'm okay, but I have two friends who are gorgeous. I'm going to get overlooked a lot, and it's all right."

"Who's your other gorgeous friend?" Jessamine asked with complete innocence. Vivian threw a pillow at her. "Me?" she asked, shocked. "Have you seen my nose?"

"Yes, it's in the center of your gorgeous face," Vivian said.

Jessamine shook her head, but she looked pleased. Was it possible she genuinely had no idea how beautiful she was? "Anyway, I'm sorry things didn't work out with my brother. He apparently has no idea what's good for him."

Vivian couldn't think of anything to say that wouldn't betray her hurt and longing so she forced a smile and focused on packing. Thankfully Jessamine didn't seem to notice. Giovanni poked his head inside the hole. "This might take longer than I thought. You can go, Jess."

"I have to take Vivian to get her car," Jessamine said.

"I'll take her," Giovanni said before disappearing again.

"Is that okay? I mean, is it weird between you guys?" Jessamine asked.

Incredibly, Vivian thought. But instead she said, "Why would it be weird? We had one casual date. It's fine, Jessamine. I see your phone buzzing out of control, and I know you have things to do. Please, go."

"Okay, but if you need anything," Jessamine said, standing to give Vivian a warm hug.

"Thank you," Vivian said, hating to have a need that compelled her to say the word so much. She liked to be self-sufficient. Relying on anyone felt like too much. Relying on her erstwhile husband's family in the midst of such awkwardness was over the top.

Jessamine left. Vivian finished packing and sat on her bed, waiting for Giovanni. He hadn't exaggerated; whatever he was doing on her roof did take a long time. Or maybe he had forgotten her. Had he driven off without her? Would she have to walk to the school to get her car? That wouldn't be a big deal normally, but it was getting dark outside, and inside, for that matter. She needed to call Annie and let her know she was coming, but her phone was almost dead and, without power, she had no way to charge it.

Maybe she should look outside and make sure Giovanni's car was still there. Dragging her suitcase down the stairs, she parked it by the entrance, flung open the door, and almost walked directly into Giovanni.

"Ready?" he asked at the same time that she said, "Sorry."

"Yes," she said, while he said, "What?"

Then there was a beat of awkward silence while each tried to catch up to what the other had said. He was standing uncomfortably close to her, closer than normal spacing allowed. Whether that was because they had almost crashed into each other or because he was a close talker, she had no idea. Had he stood so close to her at any point during *the event*? She couldn't remember. In fact, she could barely breathe. When she did breathe, she took in the earthy, sweaty smell of him. The day had been a scorcher. No doubt it was even warmer on the roof.

"Would you like a cold glass of water?" she whispered. Why was she whispering? She had no idea.

"You shouldn't open your freezer," he replied, also in a whisper. At least she wasn't the only one with panic-induced volume control. And at least they were whispering and not the other extreme. It would be beyond awkward if they were standing so close and shouting to each other. "You're smiling," he added.

"So are you," she said, amazed to see that it was true.

He moved past her and reached for her case, his bicep grazing her arm. "Ready?"

Nodding in mute assent, she followed him from the house.

CHAPTER 8

The drive to her car was silent, but not uncomfortably so. Instead of feeling awkward, the air felt charged. Vivian felt no need to break the mood with nervous chatter, and she was glad Giovanni didn't, either.

They reached the school parking lot, deserted except for her vehicle. Giovanni pulled up next to it. Vivian reached for the handle, but he put out a hand and gently grasped her wrist. "Where are you going to stay?"

"With my sister," she said.

He nodded. "You only have the one?"

"Just the one," she affirmed.

"And your parents…" he trailed off, leadingly.

"Live in North Carolina now."

Silence returned. Should she go? Was that the end of the conversation? She reached for the door again, but he was still holding her wrist. She hadn't realized until she tried to take it away. Apparently neither had he because he tugged it back again, almost possessively.

He took a breath. "I think maybe you should stay with me."

She should respond with something cool and casual. Instead she said, "Wha…?" Not even finishing the end of the word.

"Look, technically we're still married, and I have an old fashioned view of the way a woman should be taken care of. I feel really bad about everything, but mostly for dumping you off in a hotel in Gatlinburg. I shouldn't have done that; I panicked."

"Giovanni, you're really off the hook here. I told you it was my fault for buying tainted brownies from Jerry Garcia that made us lose our minds."

He chuckled. She paused to appreciate the chuckle and some of the tension between them lessened.

"I have an extra guest room and an overblown sense of guilt. It should only be for a few days and it's absolutely no trouble. I probably won't even be there most of the time. Please, unless you'd rather stay with your sister." There was a question in the last sentence.

Vivian pictured spending days at her sister's house, trapped at night in a room with her four year old niece whose overgrown adenoids made her snore like a ripsaw. She couldn't help it; she groaned a little.

"That's exactly how I would feel about staying with any of my siblings," Giovanni said. He gave her wrist a little shake. "Come on, stay with me. My guest room never gets used, which is a shame because Jessamine took so much time decorating it for me."

"Jessamine does have good taste," Vivian conceded. "But I want to be clear that I don't feel like you owe me anything. You shouldn't feel guilty. You did nothing wrong. In fact, you did everything right."

The awkwardness and tension came back full force, but this time Vivian didn't know why, at least not until Giovanni spoke. "You did a few things right, yourself."

Her jaw dropped a little before she caught it. Was he flirting with her by referencing *the event*? It appeared so. "I don't know where to go after that," she admitted, and he chuckled.

"Take it for what it is, Vivy," he said, and her heart turned over. She swallowed hard and turned to look out the window, a sinking feeling filling her gut. *I am never going to get over this man, never.* "Follow me home," he commanded, and she finally got out of the car.

His house was much like the man, buttoned down and immaculate. He had an extensive book collection and everything was in alphabetical order by author.

"How much would you kill me if I rearranged these by Dewey decimal?" she teased.

"It would be impossible to kill you after my head exploded," he said. "Are you hungry?"

Her stomach rumbled, reminding her she was famished. "Yes. Would you like to order a pizza or something? My treat."

"No need," he said and opened the refrigerator to reveal multiple foil wrapped tins. "What's your pleasure? Ravioli? Meatballs? Alfredo? I think I have some scampi in here somewhere, too."

"Um…" she said.

"My mom," he explained. "She's never quite gotten over the fact that I moved out. This is her way of compensating."

"When did you move out?" she asked.

"Six years ago," he said, and they shared a laugh.

"The Samperi's never lack for food and drama," he said. "The food I like, the drama, not so much."

"Would you like me to toss a salad?" she asked.

"No need," he said, reaching for a glass container. "Mama doesn't trust homemade salad dressing, so she always sends a week's worth of greens."

"I don't suppose she also sends you some cannoli," she said. She had tasted cannoli at Jessamine's house and never quite gotten over the experience.

"She does, but I eat that first and it's all gone. Don't tell."

"On a scale of one to ten, how terrified are you of your mother?" she asked.

"A hundred," he said. She sat idly by while he pulled down plates, arranged their food, and heated it in the microwave. Four minutes later, everything was ready. They sat across from each other at his small kitchen table. Her mind went where it shouldn't, wondering how many women over the years had occupied her same spot. Had he dated a lot of women? Probably, but she was fairly certain he hadn't married any of them.

"You're smiling again," he said.

"I'm generally a happy person," she explained.

"You're clearly not related to me," he said.

She laughed. "What are you talking about? Jessamine is a delight."

"Sure, to you. To the rest of us poor schlubs who share her DNA, she's the mean Mother Superior. And then there are my brothers."

"What's wrong with your brothers?" she asked.

"Nothing, they're just exhausting."

"How so?" she asked.

"Well, take my oldest brother, Joe. He's the perfect oldest brother with the perfect wife. They're sickeningly in love and make the rest of us look bad. Then there's my second brother, St. Benedict, who is, more often than not, off somewhere saving the world. Jessamine you know, and though you don't believe me, she can be a pain. Then there's Moss, bless him."

"Moss," she repeated. "Unusual name."

"Short for Mossimo. But you can call him Peter Pan because despite the fact that he's firmly in his twenties, everyone still treats him like he's seventeen. Mostly because he still acts like it. He still lives at home, much to our mother's delight."

"No offense, but none of that sounds bad."

"It's not, technically speaking. But we're the Yelling Samperis. Don't forget there's a reason we have that nickname. Spend twenty minutes with us and you'll be running for the earplugs and Tylenol."

She laughed because everyone did call them the Yelling Samperis. When they first arrived from Brooklyn, no one knew what to make of them. And they were *loud*. Everything seemed to be an argument with them. First people thought they were part of the witness protection program, but no one who was trying to hide would be so loud. Then people thought one or more of them must be deaf. Finally everyone realized it was how they were. They communicated by yelling.

"You don't seem like a yeller," she said.

"On my own, I'm not. But it's a family language, a sort of short-hand. Most of the time when I'm with them, I don't even realize I'm doing it. But how weird would it be if I kept it up on my own? If I went around shouting at everyone all the time?" He shuddered and she laughed again. "You're not a yeller, either," he added.

"You're not allowed to be a yeller if you're a librarian. If you have shouting tendencies or a loud voice, they come one day and drag you out of class, never to be seen or heard from again."

"Sounds intense," he said.

"The rumors are true—library science is a thug sport," she said. He laughed and had to use his napkin to cover his full mouth.

The remainder of supper was light and pleasant, and so was the cleanup after. Then they were out of tasks and the awkwardness lingered. "I'm not much into TV, but we could find something, if you like. I don't have cable, but there's PBS."

Vivian stopped herself before she could ask if he'd ever watched *Curious George*. "We could read," she suggested. "I brought a book."

"Do you take one everywhere?" he asked.

"Job hazard. You never know when there will be a library emergency and you have to catalog something."

"You're funny," he proclaimed, as if it were a revelation, which it probably was, seeing how little they knew about each other. They retrieved their books and met back in the living room. He sat on one end of the leather couch. Vivian dithered, not sure where to go. On the opposite end of the couch or the uncomfortable-looking side chair? Giovanni saved her the choice by patting the couch seat beside him. She sat.

"This is comfy," she mused.

"Thank you, my insistence paid off. Jess would have had me in some sort of mohair monstrosity. I demanded leather."

"Did she decorate all of your house?"

"Most, she has a knack," Giovanni said.

"That she does," Vivian said. Jessamine served as the family's designer, drawing up plans for her brothers to follow. She was also the client liaison and the face of the company. She craned her neck to see what he was reading. He held it up so she could get a better view. She beamed when she saw the title. "I love Teddy Roosevelt."

"Me, too," he agreed. "He's by far the best Roosevelt."

"Hear, hear," she agreed before opening her book. Unlike the last couple of weeks, she had no trouble becoming absorbed in her reading. It came as a surprise when Giovanni stretched and yawned. Vivian set her book aside and blinked sleepily at him.

"Let me show you to your room," he said. He preceded her up the stairs and set her suitcase in a room on his right. "The bathroom is across the hall, and it's all yours. I have one in my room."

"Thank you so much for this, Giovanni. You're saving me from a bedmate who snores like a wild boar."

He paused at the doorway. She turned smiling to face him, and the tension was back and heavy between them. She wished he would come inside, close the door, and tell her that he was somehow now miraculously in love with her. Barring that, she wished he would kiss her and put her out of her misery.

"Well," she said at the same time that he said, "Vivian."

"What?" they said together.

"I was probably going to thank you again," she said. She had no idea what she had intended to blurt, but she hoped it was a thank you and not some desperate plea for love. "What were you going to say?"

"I was probably going to tell you to sleep well," he said.

"We're very polite," she said.

"Aren't we, though?" he said, smiling. "I guess, goodnight." He faded into the darkness of the hallway. Vivian stood staring into the darkness, perplexed. He *guessed* good night? What did that mean?

She set her suitcase on the bed, located her nightgown and toiletries and took them into the bathroom. Though she had showered that morning, the day had been a hot and sweaty one so she showered again. Her hair didn't need another wash, so she clipped it to the top of her head and avoided the spray. After a quick—albeit refreshing—shower, she got out and scrubbed her teeth twice. Apparently Mama Samperi liked her garlic because Vivian had a mouth full of it. Her only consolation was that Giovanni probably did too, so maybe he hadn't smelled her breath. Although that was doubtful since she could probably take down a colony of vampires with one sneeze right now.

When she was finished, she glanced at herself in the mirror and frowned. Technically, *technically*, she was on her honeymoon right now. And women on their honeymoons didn't slap on an old t-shirt with a picture of a dancing unicorn on it. And they didn't scrub off their makeup. So, disregarding how silly it seemed, she reapplied some makeup to her clean face, combed through her hair, and tried to look presentable. For what, she didn't know. But at least she felt okay about herself, except for the old t-shirt. Why hadn't she thought to grab a couple of cute nighties? Because she had thought she would be sharing a room with a four year old.

Tentatively, she opened the bathroom door and stepped out. Giovanni's door was firmly closed, and she felt ridiculous for making herself up. He was in for the night. She was a houseguest and nothing more. Why was she acting like a teenager with her first crush? Straightening, she took a step toward her room when his door opened. He stuck his head out and froze at the sight of her.

"I forgot to tell you to please let me know if you need anything," he said.

"All right," she agreed. "I will. Thank you." He smiled. She smiled. They stayed that way for a minute while the tension crackled between them and then he slowly pulled his head back inside and closed his door. "Right," she said, and he opened his door again.

"Did you say something?" he asked.

"Nothing important."

"Okay," he said, and, turtle-like, went back inside again.

She took a step toward her door, paused, took another step, paused, took another step, and changed course. Before she could talk herself out of it, she was knocking on Giovanni's door.

He opened it so quickly she thought he must have been standing on the other side. "Yes?"

"I was thinking." Her fingers twined nervously together in front of her.

"Yes?" he prompted.

"Technically, we're still married..." she trailed off, suddenly struck with the horror of what she was doing. Her face flushed. She wished for another tree to fall through the house, but this time to take her out and end her misery.

"Vivian, are you propositioning me?" he said.

"I guess you could say that," she said.

"Hallelujah," he said, and this time when he closed the door and retreated inside, she was in his arms.

CHAPTER 9

As before, Vivian woke first. She lay still, a bad sense of déjà vu washing over her. The last time they were in this situation, she had felt such guilt, rejection, and humiliation. If that happened today, how would she ever face him again? He was supposed to be working on her house, which meant he was in some ways her employee. Disaster loomed on every horizon. She lay perfectly still, not wanting to wake him and find out for sure how dire things were.

His arm tightened on her waist and he pulled her closer. *Oh, sweet torture,* she thought. She chanced a glance at him and saw him blinking thoughtfully at her. "You're awake," she said stupidly.

"Nothing gets by you. Must be that master's degree," he said.

She rolled toward him and scooted as close as she dared without being obvious about it. What she really wanted was to press herself to him and absorb as much of him as she could, in case this was the last time she ever saw him. But somehow she doubted that attempting to steal his essence would be seen as anything but needy.

"Penny for your thoughts," she ventured.

"I'm your contractor now. It's going to take a lot more than that," he said, but he hooked his leg over hers and used it to pull her impossibly closer. "Speaking of which, I have to go."

Her heart sank. If this was a brushoff, it was a weird one. But what else could it be?

"You're quiet," he said.

"Not the first time someone's accused me of that," she said.

"But right now I would very much like for you to say something."

"You first," she said.

"Okay, here goes," he said, and then he kissed her and neither of them said anything for a long time. When Vivian next woke, Giovanni was gone and she had twenty minutes to get to work. She sprang out of bed in a panic, dashed down the hall to her room, threw on clothes, sprinted to the bathroom, brushed her hair, washed her face, grabbed her makeup bag, and galloped down the stairs. In her haste, she almost missed the note, but there it was underneath a travel mug of coffee he'd made for her. Beside the mug was a key to his house. She picked it up and tucked it in her purse.

"Have a pleasant day, Vivy. G." She reread the neat and tidy scrawl three times on her way out the door. That was it? He was killing her. Nonetheless she was smiling as she sauntered into work, five minutes late.

*t his work, Giovanni wore a similarly happy smile. At least until it was time to interact with his family.

"Who is this Vivian person anyway?" his younger brother, Moss, asked.

"You know her. She was a year above you in school," Jessamine said. Giovanni blinked. He hadn't known that. He assumed Vivian was from out of town. It never occurred to him they went to the same school at approximately the same time, meaning she was two years his junior. To his further chagrin, until this moment he'd had no idea how old she was. What else didn't he know about her?

"Vivian, Vivian," Moss repeated. "Doesn't ring a bell. Is she a dog?"

"She's adorable," Jessamine snapped. "Like a longhaired Kewpie doll."

"Then why don't I remember her?" Moss asked.

"Because she probably hung out with the smart kids," Jessamine said.

"Oh, that's why," Moss said. "Hey, did you hear the latest?"

"What?" Giovanni asked, anxious to change the subject.

"Benny's coming home."

"No way. Did he already save everyone in whatever South American country he's currently in?" Giovanni asked.

"He got malaria," Joe said with a snicker.

"He's coming home for malaria?" Giovanni said. "Wuss."

"Don't let Mama hear you say that," Moss said.

"I'm surprised she hasn't put a wire on you by now," Giovanni said.

"Don't give her ideas," Moss replied.

"Why would she need to wire him when the umbilical cord is still so firmly

attached?" Jessamine asked.

"Hardee, har. Moss loves his mama," Moss said. "Let's get back to this Vivian chick. Is she datable?"

"By you? No," Jessamine said. "But Benny's coming home. Maybe I'll set her up with him."

"What? Vivian is not Benny's type," Giovanni said.

"Is she a saint? Because that's his type," Joe said.

"Practically," Jessamine said and Giovanni snorted. "What?"

"Nothing. She's not Benny's type, is all," Giovanni said.

"Wait a minute. Vivian. Is this the Vivian you set the boy genius up with, only he thought it was someone else?" Joe asked, smacking Giovanni on the back of his head.

"One and the same," Jessamine said, also smacking Giovanni on the back of the head.

"Hey, concussion damage is a real thing, plus you're messing up my hair," Giovanni said.

"Now I have to meet the girl, if Giovanni rejected her and you want to pawn her off on a malaria-ridden Benny," Joe said.

"I did not reject her," Giovanni protested as Jessamine said, "I'm not trying to pawn her off; she's one of the only friends I have who I actually like."

"You could have stopped after you said, 'She's one of the only friends I have,'" Moss said and presented them with a framed photo. "I give you Vivian."

"Moss, don't touch her stuff," Jessamine said, and it was his turn to receive a smack.

"Ouch," Moss said, rubbing his head. "I was going to say that I agree with you—she's adorable, and she does look like Benny's type. I can almost picture her praying."

"Lemme see," Joe said, grabbing the frame. "Giovanni, you *idiota*."

Giovanni dodged the coming blow. "What?"

"What'd you reject her for? For some Barbie doll who probably applies makeup to vacuum?"

"I didn't reject her," Giovanni insisted.

"She said it was mutual," Jessamine added helpfully.

"It was definitely mutual," Giovanni agreed. "Really and extremely mutual."

"You don't have to sound so happy about it," Jessamine groused.

"My point is that Vivian and I are fine. We're, ah, on friendly terms."

"We all agree—Vivian is cute and nice and worthy of St. Benny. Now can we get back to work?" Joe said. "I'd like to be finished with this job by tomorrow."

"Tomorrow?" Giovanni exclaimed.

Joe spun to look at him. "You think we can get it done today?"

"No, I meant that tomorrow seems soon. Did you see the bowing on that roofline?"

"I did, and we can fix it today."

"I might have to do some intense rewiring," Giovanni said. "Might take a while."

"So you can linger after we're done here tomorrow," Joe said. "Dad's dropping off the crane and the beam any minute, so let's be ready." He clapped his hands together, ever the consummate leader and big brother. The picture of Vivian lay forgotten on her bed.

Giovanni picked it up and studied it. She was standing in front of some rock formation. Moss was right; she did look adorable. He smoothed his finger over the picture and set it on her shelf, adjusting it to a perfect forty five-degree angle before picking up his tools and getting to work.

When he arrived home at eight PM, after a fourteen-hour workday, he saw Vivian sitting at the kitchen table, her head bent over a book. Something was different, besides the woman now occupying his space.

"What's that smell?" he asked.

"Thai food," Vivian said.

My mother made Thai food? He stopped himself before he could ask the stupid question. Of course his mother hadn't made what she termed "ethnic food." "You cooked?"

"I did," Vivian said, but there was no food in sight.

"You cooked a long time ago and put it away because I didn't come home," he surmised.

"I did," she said. He didn't know her well enough to know if she was irritated, but he assumed so.

"Belatedly, I realized I didn't have your phone number to call or text and tell you when I was going to be home." He spied her phone lying on the table beside her and reached for it. "Let's remedy that." He dialed his number from her phone. "There, now I'll save you to my contacts."

Her phone beeped. She picked it up and read the text from him. **You're cute.** She smiled, and he was fairly certain he was forgiven. "Are you hungry?" she asked.

"Famished. How can I help you?"

"Just sit," she said as she stood and began preparing a plate for him. Having grown up with an overly involved Italian mother, Giovanni was used to being served, but that didn't mean he took it for granted. It was heaven to sit and have food magically appear before him, especially after such a long day.

"Would you believe me if I told you I've never eaten Thai before?" he said.

"Judging by the taste of Italy in your fridge, I would," she said.

"My mother believes that if a dish doesn't have a base of garlic and tomatoes, it's from the devil's hands," he explained.

"After tasting her food last night, I'm inclined to agree with her. But I get bored with cooking and like to branch out." She paused, blushing a little. "I have theme nights."

"Theme nights?" he asked.

"Tuesday is Thai."

"What's Wednesday?" he asked.

"Find out tomorrow," she said with a saucy little smile that made him temporarily forget his food. Then she ducked her head shyly and picked up her fork. She was still a bit of a puzzle to him. Which one was she, the shy one who seemed uncertain of her standing in the world? Or the brazen one who knocked on his bedroom door wearing only a t-shirt?

"I like Thai," he declared after a few bites of what he guessed to be peanut butter and cilantro. It was a combination he never would have configured, but somehow it worked.

"Were you working at my house all that time?" she asked. There was a bit of thankful reverence in her tone that tempted him to tell her yes, but he couldn't lie.

"No. I was at your place this morning and then I had two other jobs."

She winced. "I hate that my house has been inserted into your busyness."

He thought of his family's casual discussion of her earlier in the morning and had to fight a wince himself. "It's really no problem, we're happy to help." She opened her mouth as if to ask him a question but closed it without speaking. He could guess what she wanted to say. Had he told his family about her, about them?

"Did you talk to your sister?" he asked.

"It would have been impossible not to." She paused. "She got the impression that I was staying with Jessamine. I didn't correct her." She bit her lip, looked up at him with big eyes, and he was at a loss. She seemed to want him to say something, but he didn't know what. And he didn't know how.

They cleaned up the dishes in short order. The easy camaraderie from earlier had been replaced by a heavy sort of tension. "I'm going to shower, if you don't mind," Vivian said.

"No, please, go ahead," Giovanni said. "I take it you found the towels okay."

"Yes, they're quite fluffy."

He smiled. "Thank my sister for that. I wouldn't know from one end of textiles to another."

She laughed. "It's probably best if I don't mention to Jessamine how fluffy your towels are," she said.

He laughed weakly. "Oh, right."

There was another beat of awkwardness and then she turned and went up the stairs. Giovanni stood gazing out the window, trying to figure out if he was doing the right thing. Yesterday, seeing Vivian at the home improvement store had been like a fist to the gut, a fist that took him by surprise. He'd had no idea he would feel anything but awkwardness at seeing her again, but there had been no awkwardness, only a fierce and primal protectiveness that shot out of him so that it felt as if it were exuding from his pores. *She's mine,* had been his first thought, and that was even before he saw the man standing beside her.

Then, later, walking into her house, the smell of her, a smell he hadn't even known he remembered, had cemented everything he felt at the store. But he had never been good at words or relationships. If he had tried to explain his confusing feelings, he would have botched it. So he stayed silent and ended up blurting an invitation for her to stay with him.

At the time, he had meant it as exactly as he'd said, a remedy for lingering guilt and a way to be nice to someone in need. But then she arrived at his house, and his motives became muddled. Now everything felt unclear again. Was it a mistake to carry on a secret affair with his secret wife?

He sat and put his head in his hands, chuckling. Moss was the one who was supposed to be the screw up in their family, the one most prone to eloping with a stranger on a whim. No one would ever expect Giovanni, the Samperi's Mr. Predictable, to do something so spontaneous and ill thought. And yet that was what made it so appealing. So far things seemed to be working, but for how long? *Now what?* he thought. Had he made a mistake? Should he and Vivian have a talk and amicably decide to go their separate ways?

His phone buzzed with a text. It was from Vivian, which was odd because he could hear the water running upstairs. He picked it up and read the two words: ***Join me?***

In all the years Giovanni had lived in his house, he had never ascended the stairs so quickly.

CHAPTER 10

On Friday, Vivian drove her car into Giovanni's garage and let herself in through the kitchen. She was contemplating whether to make supper or order pizza. On the one hand, she was tired from a long day at work. On the other hand, she had about twenty bucks left until her next paycheck, unless she wanted to break into her paltry savings, which she didn't. Before she could come to a decision, she heard a key in the front door. At first she thought it was Giovanni come home early to surprise her. Then she realized he also would have used the garage. Panicked, she scrambled into the pantry and closed the door, peeking through the crack in time to see an older woman, her arms loaded with food, waltz through the kitchen door.

She's going to open the pantry, Vivian thought. *Any moment Giovanni's mother is going to open the door and see me, a strange woman, inside her son's house. There will be no way to explain and Giovanni's head will explode from sheer humiliation.*

Mama Samperi turned and walked back out of the kitchen. Vivian heard the front door open and used the opportunity to dash up the stairs. She skidded into Giovanni's room, took a quick look around, and began gathering miscellaneous items—a bottle of lotion she had left on her side of the bed and a bra she had let dry in the bathroom.

She was afraid to hide in the closet in case his mother looked in there, so she darted under the bed, breathing hard and fueled with adrenaline.

Five minutes later, when her ears strained for sounds from downstairs, Vivian saw feet walk into the bedroom. She couldn't think, couldn't even breathe. Had his mother come upstairs because she heard Vivian? Would she kneel and look under the bed, locking eyes with her unknown daughter-in-law? *I am not cut out for cloak and dagger.* But the feet never paused beside the bed. Instead they scuttled between the bathroom and the closet, and it sounded as though she was gathering things. *Does she do his laundry?* Surely not; he was twenty seven, after all.

The feet stopped, as if waiting for something, and then Vivian realized what as another pair of feet entered the room and stood in front of the bed. These feet she recognized.

"Ma, what are you doing here?" Giovanni asked.

"What do you mean? It's Friday," she said. "What are you doing home so early? And why do you keep looking around the room? Are you afraid I'm pilfering your things? You're acting funny. Are you sick?" She stepped forward and he scampered back, bumping the bed.

"Mama, I don't have a fever. I decided to have a Friday night off, is all. It's been a busy week."

"Your brother told me. You had that extra job, the Vivian woman. The one you went on a date with and didn't tell me about." When Giovanni didn't respond, she continued. "Your sister thinks she'd be a good match for Benny."

"She wouldn't," Giovanni said.

"You sound a little jealous there, son," she said, and Vivian smiled.

"Not jealous, Mama, realistic—ouch!"

"What?" his mother said.

"A bug bite, I guess," Giovanni said, rubbing the place where Vivian had plucked his leg hairs.

"You don't have bed bugs, do you? Because you go in a lot of strange houses."

"I don't have bed bugs, Ma."

"It smells different in here," she noted, sniffing.

Under the bed, Vivian tensed, but Giovanni remained silent.

"So I guess we'll see you Sunday," she continued. To Vivian, she sounded probing, even suspicious. But maybe that was her normal tone.

"See you Sunday," Giovanni replied. Satisfied, both pairs of feet vacated the room. Vivian stayed put until only one pair of feet returned. He knelt by the bed and poked his face under.

"Here, kitty, kitty," he said.

Vivian put out an arm and he used it to drag her out.

"So, that was my mom," he said.

"She seems curious," Vivian said.

"Sherlock Holmes has nothing on her."

"Does she still do your laundry?"

"Yes, but not because I want her to. Sometimes with my mother capitulation is the better course."

He sat beside her on the floor where she lay prone, staring up at him. "You're thinking things," he said.

"I'm thinking I'm a grown woman and I just hid under your bed like a naughty teenager," she said.

He sighed.

"I'm also wondering if my house will be done soon," she added.

"It was done on Wednesday," he admitted. "I didn't want to tell you. I guess that means I've been holding you here like a prisoner."

"I've been a willing victim," she said, smiling.

"Does that mean you're going home now?" he asked.

"I'm running out of clothes. People at work are going to start to talk because I'm positive the first thing people notice when they walk into school is what the librarian is wearing and whether or not it's the same thing she wore three days ago."

His eyes flicked hopefully to hers. "So maybe you're just going home to gather some things?"

"I miss my house," she said, but her hand slid out to rest on his knee. "But I would miss your house if I left now. Maybe we could come to some sort of understanding."

"Like what?" he said.

"Like maybe we visit your house during the week and my house on the weekends, sort of like a custody arrangement for dwellings," she said.

"I could cope with that. Your house and I have become good friends. I've gotten intimate with your wiring this week."

"I'll say you have," she said, and he laughed.

"Somehow I never expect you to say the things you say," he said.

"Neither do I," she admitted. She was different with him, and she liked it. "What's Sunday?"

"It's the seventh day of the week, although some people argue it's the first," he said.

"You told your mom you would see her then."

"It's family day," he explained. "We go to church and then have family dinner. It's sacrosanct. If you try to get out of it by claiming to be ill, my mother will show up with a thermometer to see if you're lying and some minestrone soup in case you're not."

She waited for him to say more, something like, "Why don't you come with me," would have been a good start. But he brushed the hair off her face and remained silent.

"I'm going out with my book club Saturday night. That includes your sister," she informed him. She had planned to skip the monthly event, but if he was going away Sunday, she thought it best to have something of her own.

He nodded. "I'll miss you."

"Tomorrow morning, maybe we could have a lie-in," she suggested.

"What's that?"

"Pajamas, pancakes, coffee, and books until our muscles begin to atrophy and we have to either get dressed or start to grow moss."

"It's a date," he said. "As long as you're the one making the pancakes. My cooking knowledge is limited to warming things up in the microwave, and even then I sometimes forget to take the fork out and end up short circuiting the kitchen."

"Not to brag, but I've been told my pancakes are killer," she said.

"Really? Who told you that?" Was that a hint of jealousy back in his tone? She blinked up at him, smiling demurely. Her four-year-old niece had been the one to gush over her pancakes, but there was no need to tell him that while he was busy picturing other men she might have cooked for.

"I thought your brother Benedict lived in another country," she said instead.

"I was hoping you forgot about that part of the conversation," he said. "Apparently he has malaria and is coming home."

"Malaria? How horrible."

"Not for Benny. He'll find a way to turn it into a cause and end up raising money for some obscure fund no one's ever heard of," Giovanni said.

"Do you two not get along?" she said.

"It's impossible not to get along with Benny, and that's the problem. Do you have any idea what it's like having a saint for a brother? He never messes up, never gets mad, never does anything wrong. It's maddening."

"I guess I should find it flattering that Jessamine thinks I'm his perfect match," she couldn't help adding.

"Only if you think being thought of as insufferably good is a compliment," he said.

"Don't you?" she asked.

"I wouldn't know; I'm not insufferably good, but then again, neither are you." He lay down beside her and propped his head on his arm.

"What? I am a very good girl, everyone says so."

"In the insanely short time I've known you, you bought a tray of questionable brownies, introduced me to my first biker bar, got me to sing karaoke in front of strangers, convinced me to marry you, and moved into my house and bedroom. According to my calculations, you're practically diabolical."

"I think you've taken gross liberties with the truth, kind sir," she said.

"Tell me one thing I said that wasn't true," he said.

"First, you were the one who suggested we get married," she said.

"After you oh-so-conveniently lost your shoe at an all night wedding chapel."

"Second, you invited me to stay with you."

"Yes, but who knocked on my bedroom door wearing nothing but a tiny t-shirt? In both cases, I was an innocent boy and you hoodwinked me with your feminine wiles."

She snuggled closer to him and sat up so that now she was the one with the upper hand. "Do you know what my feminine wiles want to do right now?"

"I don't know, but I feel a mixture of fear and elation at the prospect," he said.

She leaned closer until her lips were nearly touching his, and then she spoke. "I want to beat you to the kitchen and eat the cannoli your mom brought," she murmured before jumping to her feet and sprinting toward the stairs.

Even after taking a few seconds to regain his senses, he caught her before she reached the stairs. It was a long time before either of them made it to the kitchen.

CHAPTER 11

"*D*on't take this the wrong way, but I want to set you up with another one of my brothers."

Vivian sipped her coffee before answering, but even that didn't buy her enough time to come up with a response. "Oh."

"It's not going to be like it was with Giovanni. He and Benny couldn't be more opposite," Jessamine said.

"Benny's the good one," Vivian said.

"Saint Benny, we call him," Jessamine said. "But he's really nice looking, or so the dozens of friends who've fallen for him over the years have led me to believe. And he's stable, except for gallivanting around the globe to help people. All in all, he's a catch."

"Malaria notwithstanding," Vivian said.

"I told you he has malaria? I don't remember saying that. I must be losing it," Jessamine said.

Vivian took another sip of her coffee. Giovanni had told her about Benny's malaria, but it wasn't as if she could explain that.

"Anyway, he won't be home for a while because he has to get well enough to be able to fly or something, so you have time to think about it," Jessamine said. "I promise I won't let another one of my brothers hurt you."

"Giovanni didn't hurt me," Vivian said, which she belatedly realized was only half true. His initial rejection had hurt, but he had done a lot in the past week to make up for it.

"What's that smile for?" Jessamine asked.

"My mind wandered, sorry."

"Don't tell me it wandered to the book. This month's selection was a dud," Jessamine said, holding the copy of their club's book selection aloft.

"No argument here," Vivian said. The other members of their group had gone home after the discussion, but it had become their habit to linger over coffee and talk. Vivica was usually with them, but she was fighting the flu. "What are your family dinners like?"

"Boisterous and coma-inducing from so much food. You should come sometime."

"Outsiders are allowed?" Vivian asked.

Jessamine laughed. "It's not a cult, Vivian."

"Are you Catholic?" Vivian asked, feeling no small amount of embarrassment that she didn't know this large and looming detail about the man she had married. If Giovanni was Catholic, and they stayed married, would she have to convert?

"We used to be," Jessamine said.

"What changed?"

"Are you sure you want to hear? It's a long story."

"Your family fascinates me," Vivian said.

Jessamine laughed again. "Then you need to get out more. Anyway, my great grandfather was the first Samperi in the US. He came ahead of my grandmother to find a job and get settled. When he did, he sent for her. This was back in the thirties when immigrants were still coming through Ellis Island, and they had a bunch of rules, namely that you couldn't be sick. That wasn't a problem until there was a polio outbreak on the ship. Everyone who had it got sent back; everyone who was suspect got put into quarantine, including my eighteen-year-old great grandmother. She was young and alone, had a fever, and only spoke Italian, so you can imagine her panic. Well, this was when polio was feared like the plague. No one knew how you got it and it had no cure, so she became a pariah. None of the other Italian-speaking Catholics would have anything to do with her. The only people who would come near her were the Methodists from England. And not only did they come near her, they laid hands on her and prayed for a miracle. The next day, her fever broke. The day after that, my grandfather was allowed to take her home. The first thing she said to him was that, in America, they were going to be Methodists."

"And he agreed?" Vivian asked.

"On the condition that his mother in Italy never find out. And she never did. So that's why the Samperis are Methodists."

"Was your mom Methodist when she married your dad?"

"Oh, no, she was Catholic. It didn't go over well with her family at all that she wanted to leave the church. There was a struggle for a while. I don't remember it, but I guess when Joe was little he split his time between being an altar boy at Mass and going to Sunday School. It probably would have come to a head, because he was nearing confirmation, but we moved here. And, as fate would have it, there aren't a lot of Catholics in this part of Kentucky, but there sure are a lot of Methodists. We fit right in."

Vivian wasn't sure if she was being sincere or sarcastic because the Samperis did anything but fit in. Besides being loud, they were all beautiful. And then there was the accent and their mad remodeling skills.

"How did you come to be builders?" Vivian asked.

"We've always been handy. Must be in the genes or something. But come on, Vivian, you don't want to spend the whole night talking about my family. What's new with you?"

I'm living with your brother now because I'm secretly your sister-in-law, but we're choosing not to tell people for reasons that are becoming less clear to me. "Not much. Did I tell you about the guy from work?"

"The one I met at Home Depot?"

"Right. His wife officially filed for divorce and he seems to be trying to use me to ease the hurt."

"Uh-oh."

"For sure. I don't know how to tell him I'm not interested. I'm not good at this sort of thing."

"Are you sure you're not interested? Despite the baggage, he was really cute."

"I'm beyond positive, and the last thing I want to do is lead him on."

"Then I see nothing for it but to be up front with him, if he keeps pursuing you. And judging by his proprietary attitude on Monday, he's going to keep pursuing you."

"Proprietary attitude?"

"Oh, come on. You didn't notice how upset he got when Giovanni took over the tarps? He had been hoping to swoop in and rescue you, and then my dumb brother intervened. Although, if you don't like the guy, then I suppose it was convenient that Giovanni intruded."

"Convenient, yes," Vivian agreed.

"How did it go after I left? Was it awkward? I felt bad."

"Don't feel bad, please. It wasn't awkward. Giovanni is a very nice man. It was so great of all of you to fix my house."

"Did Giovanni finally get it done? I was going to call you Wednesday morning and tell you it was ready, but he said he found a wiring problem and it was going to be a while. I hope he didn't hold you up from getting back in there. Was it awful staying with your sister?"

"I had a great week. Really. I'm still waiting on my bill, though."

Jessamine gave her a blank look. "But I checked with Joe and he said it's been paid. He said you gave the money to Giovanni."

"Oh, oh, right, duh." She tapped her head. "Guess I need to cut back on the caffeine."

"I thought you got decaf," Jessamine said suspiciously, sounding a whole lot like her mother.

"Right, well then maybe I need more caffeine. So what's going on with you?"

Jessamine looked around and leaned closer. "Can you keep a secret?"

Boy, can I, Vivian thought. She nodded.

"I applied to be on a television show."

"You're kidding me," Vivian said, her furtive whisper matching Jessamine's. "Which one?"

"A new decorating show on the home and garden channel. Joe would flip if he found out, but probably nothing will come of it and he'll never know."

"Jess, that's huge, and it would be so awesome."

"I know, right? And I know I'm prejudiced, but can't you picture my brothers on TV? It's like they were made for it. Sturdy, reliable Joe, St. Benedict, geek-chic perfectionist Giovanni, and loveably cute Moss."

"Not to mention their stunningly beautiful sister who basically runs the show and tells them all what to do."

Jessamine rolled her eyes, but she was smiling. "It would be huge for our business, and my brothers would go viral, I know it."

Vivian's smile faded. If that was true, it could mean millions of female fans for Giovanni. *Her* Giovanni.

"What?" Jessamine asked.

"Nothing."

"No, really, Vivian, what? I want to hear differing opinions."

"I'm not sure it's a differing opinion, because I still think it would be an amazing opportunity. But the realist in me is thinking about the invasion of privacy."

Jessamine smiled again. "You've clearly never met my family if you think we have any privacy. My mother's motto is, 'If you've got a secret, then I wasn't trying hard enough to find it.'"

Vivian laughed weakly.

"Speaking of my mother, she wants to meet you. Are you okay?"

Vivian spluttered a sip of coffee all over herself. "Why does she want to meet me?" she asked as she began mopping her shirt.

"I told you—she likes to have her finger on the pulse of the Samperi family. You had a date with Giovanni, we fixed your house, and now I want to set you up with Benny. You're practically one of us, which means any day now she'll probably start stuffing your fridge with food and doing your laundry."

"She does everyone's laundry?"

"Oh, sure. You don't think an almost thirty year old is capable of doing it him/herself, do you? And we all hate it, except Moss who probably still sucks his thumb and sleeps with a teddy bear."

"What about the married one, Joe?"

Jessamine raised an eyebrow. "Let's just say my sister-in-law is a patient, tolerant woman."

"Wow," Vivian said.

"Yep, and then she wonders why all the rest of us are still single. Not to say she's not a good woman, though. She's the best—loyal, caring, nurturing. Sometimes a little too much, you know?"

"Not really. My parents moved away as soon as my sister and I were out of the nest. In my dad's words, 'Fly, little birdies, your mom and I are hitting the beach.'"

"I'd have to believe that's healthier," Jessamine said.

"Also lonelier," Vivian admitted. "Especially for my sister. I think she has some bitterness about raising her kids sans their grandparents."

"At least she has you," Jessamine said.

"Yeah, but I have to admit I'm not the most involved aunt. I love them, but they're so...needy. And I know nothing about children, *nothing*. Wow, saying that out loud makes me sound petty and selfish. Sorry."

Jessamine shook her head. "Don't worry about it, although I have to tell you I absolutely cannot wait to have nieces and nephews."

"What about kids of your own?"

"I repeat: I cannot wait to have nieces and nephews."

They shared a laugh. "Pregnancy, childbirth, and motherhood are no joke," Vivian mused. "Seeing my sister go through it really de-glamorized the whole process for me."

"We're young and unattached. By the time we find someone and settle down, we could be in our thirties before we have kids. Maybe we'll be ready by then."

Or with one slip-up, I could get pregnant at any moment, Vivian thought, and it was enough to almost make her hyperventilate. In all the week's excitement, she hadn't once factored children into it. What would they do if she accidentally got pregnant?

"Are you okay? You look a little green," Jessamine said.

"Thinking about having kids does that to me sometimes," Vivian said.

Jessamine patted her shoulder. "Ease up, Vivian. It's practically light years away for you."

"Yeah," Vivian agreed lamely. She wasn't late, was she? She hadn't looked at the calendar much lately, and she had sort of lost track of things. "I should probably go."

"Okay, are you all right to drive home?"

"Absolutely," Vivian said. "I'm a little tired, that's all."

"You probably didn't get much sleep this week," Jessamine said.

"What? Why would you say that?"

"Because you were at your sister's," Jessamine said, and now she was really looking at her strangely.

"Right. Yes, sleeping in someone else's bed always has that effect on me. I'll see you, Jessamine. Keep me informed about the s-h-o-w."

"Who exactly are you spelling that for?" Jessamine asked.

"The walls might have ears," Vivian said.

"Only when my mother's around," Jessamine said. "And, hey, keep in mind that you're invited to Samperi Sunday anytime."

"I might take you up on that someday," Vivian said.

"See that you do, preferably right after Benny gets home," Jessamine said with a happy little wave goodbye.

At home, Vivian let herself in with a feeling of dread. She hadn't seen Giovanni's car out front. Had reality finally settled in? Had he gone home? But, no, he sat at her kitchen table dismantling her toaster oven.

"This toaster oven was a fire hazard," he explained. "I'm fixing a short."

"I'll be right back." She sprinted to her room and checked the calendar she kept in her bedside drawer. She wasn't late, and she breathed an audible sigh of relief before meandering back downstairs.

She pushed aside the toaster oven, sat in Giovanni's lap, and kissed him. "Thank you," she said when the kiss was finished.

"It was only a toaster oven, but you're welcome."

"Jessamine told me you paid for my repair." He couldn't know how very tight her finances were, but Vivian did. Worry had been gnawing her since the tree fell.

"What are husbands for?" It was the first time he referred to himself as her husband, and her heart turned over.

"I could show you later, if you like," she said.

"Woman, you are wearing me out. And for that I'm extremely grateful," he said. "Did you and Jess have a good time?"

"We did."

"Did she tell you about the TV show?" he asked.

"She said it was a secret."

"Sweetness, the Samperis have no secrets," he said. "Except one, and she's all mine." He gave her a squeeze and tucked a wayward strand of hair behind her ear. "You know what's weird?"

"People who make life choices based on the Kardashians?"

"Yes, but I was leading somewhere with my question."

"Sorry, go ahead," she said.

"A week ago, I sat at home by myself and read a book, and I was supremely happy. Tonight I sat at your table by myself and worked on a toaster oven, and I was lonely and bored."

"You must really hate toaster ovens," she said. "Or something."

"Or something," he agreed.

"You want to hear my something weird?"

"Please," he said.

"This is the first time I have ever left book group before the coffee shop closes two hours from now. I think your sister thinks I may be coming down with mono."

"So, since we have some free time, what do you do for fun at casa Vivian?" he asked.

"How do you feel about Scrabble?" she asked.

"I have no personal feelings about it, but I should warn you that Samperis are inherently competitive," he said.

"You don't know competitive until you've seen a gaggle of librarians on a Scrabble bender," she said.

"The fact that you used 'gaggle' in everyday life tells me I might be in trouble, but I'm willing to take the chance," he said.

"Famous last words," she said and retrieved her Scrabble board.

CHAPTER 12

*B*y the time Halloween rolled around, Vivian and Giovanni had started to settle into their new lives. Both were creatures of habit, so neither had trouble easing into a routine that worked for them. On Monday through Thursday they slept at Giovanni's house. On Friday morning, Vivian woke early to scrub any signs of herself from his house. It worked in their favor that Mama Samperi was also a creature of habit, so that by the time she came for her weekly Friday visit, all traces of Vivian's presence had been erased. Vivian was a meticulous, detailed sort of person anyway, but fear of discovery by her still unknown mother-in-law was even more inducement not to leave any evidence of herself behind.

On the weekends, they stayed at Vivian's house. Though Vivian had always loved her own space, she liked Giovanni's house, too, and knew he felt the same about her house. It helped that they were both busy with work, and then on Sundays Vivian went to visit her sister while Giovanni had his own family day. They hadn't had an argument yet, and while Vivian thought this was a good thing, she wondered if it spoke to deeper issues in their relationship. Some days she felt like they were merely dating, and the shallowness of their situation was beginning to wear on her. Somehow, and with no discussion, they had agreed on a set of unspoken rules. Rule number one was that they never went out in public together. Their first date had so far been their only date. She hadn't mentioned as much to Giovanni because she didn't want to upset the status quo, but as time went on, she began to wonder if things would ever change. Rule number two was to keep things secret, and Vivian began to wonder why. Was Giovanni ashamed of their dubious beginnings? Or, worse, was he ashamed of her? Did he not see a future for them? Was their current situation a test run? All in all, Vivian felt insecure, a feeling she hated. She had never been that woman, and yet now she was.

Halloween fell in the middle of the week, and they switched up their routine so Vivian could be home. Giovanni had never given out candy, but for Vivian the day was a highlight. She looked forward to dressing up like a cat and handing out candy to the kids in her neighborhood. It was one of her favorite events of the year. She had hoped Giovanni would join her, either at the door or sitting on the porch, but instead he sat on her couch and watched a game. Since this was the first bit of sports he had watched since they met, she couldn't begrudge him, even if she was secretly disappointed.

After the first round of kids, she sat beside him and waited for more.

"Why don't you have a real cat?" He was staring intently at the game, so it came as something of a surprise when he spoke.

"I'm allergic," she explained. "Why don't you?"

"My wife's allergic," he said, and she smiled.

"I like it when you call me your wife," she said.

He took her hand and kissed the back of it, still not taking his eyes off the TV. "Statement of fact, Vivy."

Suddenly Vivian was in the mood to talk more, but it wasn't the time. She contented herself with holding his hand and staring at his profile until another round of kids rang the bell. He was a sincerely handsome man, if one liked intelligent-looking men who wore glasses. Lucky for Vivian, she did.

When she returned to the couch, it was halftime. Giovanni stretched and yawned and finally turned to look at her.

"Have you ever been close to marriage before?" she asked.

He blinked at her, reorienting his mind from sports. "No, never. I've dated casually a bit, but I like my space and my routine. I might never have gotten married if some vixen hadn't drugged me with brownies and kidnapped me to Gatlinburg."

Vivian rolled her eyes. He liked to tease her about their origins. Sometimes she rose to the bait, and sometimes she didn't. Tonight she wasn't in the mood.

"How about you? Have you ever gotten close?" he asked.

"Not really. In high school, I had a boyfriend. We had been friends for a long time, and we were in marching band together. I played the trumpet and he played the sousaphone. Even though we were only seventeen, things were getting serious. We decided to go to the same college." She paused.

"What happened?" he prompted.

"A month before graduation, he was killed in a car accident." Unbidden, she burst into tears and swiped them furiously away, embarrassed. "I'm sorry, I haven't cried about it in years. I don't know why I'm crying about it now. I guess maybe Halloween reminds me of him—our senior year we went together, and it was the last time I went trick-or-treating." Self-conscious, she reached for a tissue.

He gathered her close and held her tightly. "I'm sorry, Vivian. I'm sure it still hurts to think about losing someone you loved. You shouldn't be embarrassed about a few cleansing tears every now and then. What was his name?"

"Trent," she said, sniffling. Now that the floodgates were open, she was having a hard time closing them again. For so long, she had shunned getting close to anyone for fear that they would disappear like he had. "I rather avoided men after he died. I might never have cozied up to commitment, if some guy hadn't abducted me and taken me to Gatlinburg on his motorcycle."

"Sadness has addled your brain, sweetness," he said, patting her. She gave a tremulous laugh. "Can I tell you something?"

"Anything," she said.

"When you cry, it's like someone is using a cheese grater on my heart. So if you could never shed tears again, that would be awesome," he said.

"I'll try, but you know women cry sometimes because we're happy, and sometimes for no reason at all. I'm sure you picked some of this up from your sister."

"Not really. Sometimes I think Jess is more of a guy than I am," he said.

The doorbell rang and Giovanni checked his watch. "The time for trick-or-treat is over. Go kick them to the curb."

"You're a Halloween Grinch," she said.

"And proud of it," he said and turned his attention back to the game.

Vivian opened the door and saw her niece and nephew on the step. "Trick-or-treat, Aunt Vivian," her niece said, holding a cloth pumpkin aloft for candy.

"Oh, my," Vivian exclaimed.

"You talked me into taking the kids out this year," Annie said proudly. "You were right, it's been so much fun. But now Gertie has to use the potty."

Gertie danced from toe to toe to illustrate the point.

"All right," Vivian said, but her mind was a blank.

"Uh, Vivian, can you move aside so she can get in?" Annie asked.

"Um, sure," Vivian said. She slipped aside as Gertrude dashed by, followed by Annie and two-year-old Bowden.

Maybe this is for the best, Vivian thought. Keeping the secret from her sister had grown wearisome. In fact, the more she thought about it, the more anxious she was to unburden herself. "Come all the way in." She grasped Annie's wrist and pulled her into the living room, presenting the small space with almost a flourish.

"You were watching sports?" Annie asked.

Vivian couldn't believe it. Giovanni had disappeared. Annie stepped closer and narrowed her eyes. "Have you been crying?"

"You know how I feel about sports," Vivian said.

"Vivian, what's going on?" Annie asked.

"I was thinking about Trent," Vivian admitted.

"Wow, I haven't heard you mention him in forever," Annie said. She sat. "Look, Vivian, I know how you are."

"How am I?"

"Loyal. Once a person is your person, they are always your person. But Trent is gone. You need to open yourself up to the possibility of someone else."

"You're right."

"What?"

"I said I agree with you."

"I'm not sure you've ever said that before," Annie said. "Do you have anyone in mind?"

"Well…"

"Because I do."

"What? Who?" Vivian asked.

"Bob McGregor from church."

"Annie, he's old."

"He's forty," Annie said.

"He's weird," Vivian countered.

"He's not that weird," Annie said.

"His name is Mr. McGregor," Vivian said.

"So?"

"So who am I, Peter Rabbit? I don't even like to garden."

"Vivian, I know you."

"Why do you keep saying that like I'm some sort of government experiment gone wrong?"

"You could never date someone young and stupid, someone messy or lazy or addicted to sports or video games."

"Don't you think there are any men who fit that description who were also born after the polio vaccine was invented?" Vivian asked.

"Maybe, but you'll never give them a chance because you're afraid."

"What do you think I'm afraid of?"

"Change. Commitment. Failure."

"Well, I guess you have me all wrapped up," Vivian said.

"Tell me where I'm wrong," Annie demanded.

Vivian opened her mouth and closed it again. She couldn't very well blurt the truth of Giovanni with Giovanni lurking nearby. Although this would be a perfect time for him to make an entrance on his own…

He didn't, though. Gertrude emerged from the bathroom and, after some feeble attempts at small talk, Annie and the kids left. Giovanni finally appeared from his hiding place—Vivian never figured out where—and sat on the couch, resuming his game without a word. Meanwhile Vivian stewed. She got why he didn't want to tell his family, but why couldn't they tell hers?

Her phone rested on the table beside her. She picked it up and sent a text.

Is your invitation still on for Samperi Sunday?

Jessamine responded immediately.

Yes! And your timing couldn't be better because * drumroll * Benny's home.

Vivian set the phone down with a satisfied smile. Giovanni liked secrets. She could have secrets, too.

Later that night they lay in bed, Vivian reading until her eyelids drooped. She thought Giovanni was already asleep until he wrapped his arm around her, pulled her close, and whispered, "Goodnight, Mrs. McGregor."

And that was why, for the first time, Vivian kicked him in the shin.

CHAPTER 13

On Sunday morning, Giovanni kissed Vivian goodbye. "See you later, sweetness."

Sooner than you know, Vivian thought. But she didn't say it. She kissed him sweetly goodbye and stood waving at the door with her coffee. After he was gone, she dashed upstairs and dressed with care, making sure her makeup, hair, and outfit were perfect. She would be meeting Giovanni's family for the first time and, whether they knew it or not, it was a momentous occasion.

"Hey, you look extra pretty today," Annie said when Vivian slid into the pew beside her at church. "Any particular reason?" Her eyes slid to Bob McGregor.

"Stop it," Vivian said.

"He has a house and a nice car," Annie whispered.

"Yes, but does he have any of his original teeth?" Vivian asked.

"He's only fourteen years older than you," Annie said.

"And only fourteen years younger than our dad," Vivian retorted.

Annie made a face. "I hadn't considered that. Still, there has to be someone out there for you."

"Keep the dream alive," Vivian said, and the service began. After church, Vivian begged off Annie's lunch invitation and, with shaking hands, drove toward the Samperi's estate. Even from far away, it was an impressive sight.

Upon his arrival in Kentucky, Mr. Samperi bought a massive rattletrap horse barn and converted it into living quarters for his family. He did such an impressive job, and the project drew so much interest from the community, that he had an almost instantaneous new career as a remodeler. Back when he was the only one working, he had more business than he could handle. Now three of his sons and a daughter were involved, and they still had almost more than they could handle. Eventually, when his kids became teenagers and started taking up some of the slack in his workload, he was able to turn his attention to building the family a house. Again, the house drew so much speculation that it landed on the cover of a magazine, and the Samperis branched from remodeling, to building to everything in between. All in all, Vivian guessed they had to be loaded, although she had no idea because she and Giovanni had never discussed money. She still paid for her own house, utilities, gas, and groceries, and so did he. Sometimes when they ordered pizza he paid, and sometimes she did. Since she had no idea how married couples worked, she had no idea if they were normal. She suspected not. And when she thought about discussing their finances, she felt queasy. When that happened, she would have to tell Giovanni how dire her money situation was. She didn't want to because she was embarrassed and a little ashamed of her debt. Between the loans she had accrued for her bachelor's degree, followed by more loans for her graduate degree, along with her car loan and a mortgage, she would probably never be out of debt. Part of her felt like she had done something wrong with her money; the other part couldn't figure out what she could have done differently. As she drove up the Samperi's long lane, she pushed all thoughts of money from her mind.

Jessamine greeted her at the door of the house with a warm hug. "You made it. I'm so glad you're here."

"Me, too," Vivian said, although she sounded uncertain. Still, it was worth it to catch a peek inside the beautiful home. Though it was relatively new, it had been built to match the barn so that it was a rambling six-bedroom Victorian with all the requisite architectural details. "I cannot believe your dad built this all by himself."

"We Samperis may not have a lot going for us, but we're handy with a hammer," Jessamine said. "And we're loud. Prepare yourself." Her hand lingered on the door as she gave Vivian the warning.

"I'm ready," Vivian said, although she wasn't sure she meant it. Her heart was about to thud out of her chest cavity and she regretted eating a piece of toast with her coffee that morning.

The door opened and she questioned how many people could possibly be inside. It sounded like the cheering section at a Big Ten football game. "And there aren't even any kids yet. Can you imagine what it's going to be like when we start adding nieces and nephews?" Jessamine said, shouting to be heard over the din. "Come meet everyone." She took Vivian's hand and led her to an attractive-looking man and woman. The man was yelling something to someone across the room, but the woman was quiet.

"This is my sister-in-law, Peaches," Jessamine introduced. "Peaches, this is Vivian."

"Hi," the woman said with a smile that lit her face. "Peaches isn't my real name, by the way," she explained, but Vivian never got to hear what her real name was because the man next to her stopped yelling and turned to face her.

"You must be Vivian," he said and put out a hand that dwarfed Vivian's with its enormity and grip. He was by far the largest of the Samperis, a virtual bear of a man, not fat, but tall and broad. Beyond his size, he exuded a sort of magnetic power that Vivian was sure would make people want to do whatever he told them to do.

"You must be Joe," she said.

"If you say so, then I must," he said and gave her a half smile that was boyishly charming. If she didn't know better, she might think him a little shy, but his nose had been broken twice and healed crooked, giving him a tough, roguish appearance.

"So this is Vivian," said another voice to her left, and right away Vivian knew he must be Mossimo, the youngest. His hair was a messy mop of curls. He wore a t-shirt with the name of some band on it, and his feet were encased in a well-worn pair of Converse. All in all he looked more seventeen than twenty-five, but he was cute and also smiling at her.

"Hello," she said, and now she was the one who sounded shy. Moss was the closest to her in age and his interested appraisal told her he wasn't ignorant of that fact.

"Come meet my dad," Jessamine said, expertly shepherding Vivian away from her eager little brother. "Pete Samperi, this is my friend, Vivian Haslett."

"Welcome, Vivian," Mr. Samperi boomed but despite his big voice, he was a small man, far shorter and slimmer than any of his sons.

"Your house is beautiful, Mr. Samperi," Vivian declared.

"Thank you, Miss Vivian. Marie!" The shout was so sudden that Vivian flinched.

Mrs. Samperi stuck her head out of the kitchen. "What is it?" She yelled, though they were no more than five feet apart.

"It's Jessamine's friend, Vivian," Mr. Samperi yelled, and now another head appeared from the kitchen. Giovanni blinked at Vivian, his mouth puckered in surprise.

"Well, come into the kitchen," Mrs. Samperi called before disappearing back the way she came.

"That's like being invited into the inner sanctum," Mr. Samperi said, patting Vivian lightly on the shoulder. Jessamine led Vivian to the kitchen, a room that was approximately half the size of Vivian's house.

"Mama, this is Vivian Haslett," Jessamine introduced. "And Giovanni you know." She gestured halfheartedly toward Giovanni who stood with his back leaning against the counter.

"Hi, Giovanni," Vivian said, giving him a little wave. He nodded at her, but his mouth was twisted in a repressed smile, so she knew she was forgiven for surprising him. "Mrs. Samperi, it smells amazing in here."

"Thank you, dear," Mrs. Samperi said distractedly.

"How can I help you?" Vivian asked and suddenly she could hear a pin drop as it seemed the entire house came to a standstill as everyone stopped and stared at Vivian.

"What did she say?" Moss asked, poking his head in the door.

"Nothing," Jessamine said, shoving him out again. "Mom doesn't allow anyone to help in the kitchen," she explained to Vivian.

"Oh, I'm sorry," Vivian said, feeling uncertain and more than a little embarrassed.

"Nonsense," Mrs. Samperi said. "Never apologize for good manners, Vivian. And I certainly do let people help me in the kitchen."

Giovanni snorted as Jessamine muttered, "Yeah, right."

Mrs. Samperi set down her spoon and put her hands on her hips. "All right, I'll prove it. Vivian, I have a job for you, if you don't mind, dear."

"Anything," Vivian said.

"I'm going to prepare a tray for my other son, Benedict. He's not well. Would you mind very much taking it up to him?"

"Ma," Giovanni said.

"I'd be delighted," Vivian interjected.

Mrs. Samperi smiled and set about preparing a tray. "The kids tell me you went to school with them, but I don't recall hearing them mention you until recently," she said.

"I was sandwiched between Moss and Giovanni," Vivian explained.

"And you never crossed paths?" Mrs. Samperi said.

"Well, to be honest, I had a pretty big crush on Giovanni, but he was a senior and I was a lowly sophomore," Vivian said.

"You never told me that," Giovanni said. He leaned toward Vivian, his elbows resting on the slab of granite that separated them.

"It's not exactly the kind of thing you mention on a casual first date, Giovanni," Vivian said. "Unless you're a weirdo."

"And you're certainly not a weirdo, Vivian," he said. "Wildly unpredictable, but not a weirdo."

Vivian was aware that Jessamine and Mrs. Samperi were both watching them so she forced a bland smile and leaned back, disengaging from Giovanni.

"Here you go, dear," Mrs. Samperi said. "It's the third room on the right at the top of the stairs. Thank you." She shoved a loaded tray toward Vivian.

"Can you carry that?" Giovanni asked.

"Don't pander to stereotypes, son. It's not politically correct," Mrs. Samperi said. "I'd guess Vivian is much stronger than she looks."

The tray was heavy and awkward, but what could Vivian say after that? Smiling, she picked up the tray and headed for the stairs. By the time she reached the top, she was winded and her arms shook from exertion. Using her foot to knock, she tapped lightly on the partially closed door.

"I'm not hungry, Ma," a weak voice called.

Vivian poked her head around the door. "Would you mind if I came in and set this down? Otherwise I'm going to drop it all over your mother's spotless hallway, and even though I've just met her, I think she may find it an unforgiveable offense."

"Sure, come in. Sorry, I thought you were my mom, but you're clearly not," Benny said as Vivian eased into the room and set the tray on the table beside his bed.

"I'm Vivian," she said.

"Are you a nurse or an angel?" he asked. He looked quite ill, like someone who used to be robust but had recently lost a lot of weight. He lay uncomfortably in the bed and his skin had a sickly yellowish cast to it.

"Neither," she said.

"You're too pretty to be a nun, but I can't imagine anyone else my mom would send up with food," he said.

"You can call me Sister Vivian, if it would make you feel better. Can I help you with some of this? It looks like a lot to tackle." Her hand waved over the massive mound of food.

"My mother doesn't take no for an answer when it comes to food, but I'm genuinely not hungry."

"I'm desperately trying to make a good impression on your mother, and it would really help me out if I could get you to eat something. How about three bites and a few sips of lemonade? I mean, everyone likes lemonade."

"Are you in sales, Vivian?" He struggled to sit up. Vivian reached forward to help him by propping several pillows behind him.

"I'm a librarian," she said. She perched on the edge of his bed and held the lemonade for him while he drank a healthy amount.

"Why is a pretty librarian bringing me food and trying to impress my mother?" he asked.

"It's a secret," she said.

"Am I actually awake, or is this another hallucination?"

She pinched his arm, albeit lightly, and then fed him a bite of what she guessed to be minestrone soup.

"When you feed me, the soup actually tastes good. Must be angel magic," he said.

"I'm no angel," she said. "Just an ordinary woman who gives of her time to feed missionaries recovering from malaria."

"That's a specific line of work you're in," he said.

"What country were you in?" she asked.

"Suriname," he said.

"The smallest country in South America," she commented.

"Seriously, who are you?" he asked. "No one ever has any idea where Suriname is. I've been tempted to make up cards explaining that it's not in Africa." After finishing the bowl of minestrone, he took another sip of lemonade and put up his hand when she tried to offer him more.

"I'm a person who enjoys a good game of trivia now and then," she said. "For instance, I know Suriname has an awfully high poverty rate and that pediatric AIDS is ravaging the country."

He glanced down at the tray and remained silent.

"I'm guessing malaria wasn't the worst thing you encountered there," she said, her tone gentle. "Here, have a piece of chocolate." She unwrapped the piece of gold foil chocolate his mother had lovingly placed on his tray and put it in his palm. After staring at it a few seconds, he popped it in his mouth like medicine. "You should rest now, you look exhausted."

"I can't sleep," he admitted with the chagrined tone of someone not used to voicing complaints. "My joints hurt and nothing feels comfortable."

"I think I can help you. When my sister was hugely pregnant, I did a lot of research to see which sleeping position took the most weight off the sciatic nerve. Do you mind if I position you? It's going to involve touching."

"I don't mind, but even if I did, I'm too weak to protest much," he said. He watched while she rolled him onto his left side, readjusted his limbs, and propped a pillow between his knees. "That does feel better," he admitted, but his eyes remained open and hollow. Vivian guessed his insomnia might have more to do with a few waking nightmares than any physical discomfort. Suddenly she felt incredibly sorry for him. In addition to the malaria that had ravaged his body, he looked like something had ravaged his soul. And though she was new to the family, so far he felt the most like a brother.

"Would you like me to read to you?"

He smiled, amused by the offer. "If you like."

She stood and retrieved a copy of *The Lion, The Witch, and the Wardrobe* she had noticed when she first walked into the room. Judging by the well-worn cover, she guessed it was a favorite of his. She read two chapters before she perceived he was snoring softly. As silently as possible, she stood and tiptoed from the room.

The family was gathering around the table as she eased into the room. It was a massive table, no doubt custom built by Mr. Samperi or one of his sons. Had Giovanni had a hand in it? It gave her a ridiculous thrill to know that he was able to make something out of nothing. She had never had the ability to create that way, and she admired people who did.

"How's Benny?" Mrs. Samperi asked.

"He ate the soup, drank the lemonade, and now he's sleeping," Vivian said and, once again, everyone came to a standstill and watched her.

"I don't think he's slept since he got home," Mr. Samperi said.

"He's a lot sicker than we realized," Jessamine explained in a worried voice.

"I haven't been able to get him to eat a thing," Mrs. Samperi said, and she sounded near tears. "Thank you, Vivian."

"It was nothing," Vivian said, embarrassed. "This looks delicious." She turned her attention to the groaning table and, thankfully, everyone else did the same. They had saved her a seat between Jessamine and Giovanni. She sat, and Mr. Samperi prayed. She liked the way he prayed, plainspoken and with confidence. And he mentioned her, their new friend Vivian who got Benny to eat and wasn't intimidated by Jessamine. Everyone laughed at that, and then it was time to eat.

The food was passed from left to right with everyone taking generous portions of everything. Vivian had no idea how the other women maintained their figures. Then again, they were all taller than she was. She tried to take tiny portions without drawing attention to herself. It was hard to pass up the shrimp scampi. It was her favorite dish that Mrs. Samperi sent to Giovanni's, and she only made it occasionally. Still, she needed to be strong if she planned to fit in her pants this time next year. She took a tiny portion and passed it along. Giovanni took it and, without looking at her, added another scoop to her plate. *I love, love, love this man*, she thought and, strangely, it was the first time she had admitted as much, even to herself. Up to this point she hadn't let herself think about where they were or where they were going. Instead she had focused on making the most of each day. But here, in his original home and with his family, she couldn't deny the truth any longer; she was completely and totally in love with her husband. The knowledge made her almost giddy. Was this how people in arranged marriages felt? She wondered.

"So, Vivian, tell us about yourself. What's your family like?" Mrs. Samperi asked.

"My parents were teachers and are now retired. They're fulfilling their dream of living by the ocean. I have an older sister. She's married and has two kids, a boy and a girl."

"Your parents must love having grandbabies," Mrs. Samperi said. To her right, Peaches froze mid-bite and so did Joe.

"I think it was a bit of a shock, actually. My parents had kids young, but I don't think they expected their kids to do the same."

"How old was your sister when she had her first baby?" Mrs. Samperi asked.

"Twenty five."

"Can you believe some twenty five year olds are still living with their parents?" Jessamine asked with a significant look at Moss.

"Can you believe some thirty year olds are still unmarried?" he shot back.

"Children," Giovanni reprimanded.

"Do you and your sister bicker, Vivian?" Mrs. Samperi asked.

"Only when we're awake," Vivian said, earning her a smile from the elder Samperis.

After supper, Vivian's request to help clean up was denied so Jessamine took her on a tour of the barn.

"What do they do with it now that everyone is either gone or living in the main house?" Vivian asked.

"Nothing. It's kind of sad, actually. Most of our memories happened out here. I mean, the house is nice, but it doesn't feel like home as much as this does."

"It's spectacular," Vivian admired. While the home was large and impressive, the barn was homey and warm. She could imagine all the rambunctious little Samperis scuttling around, wrestling, shouting, and generally driving their parents up a wall. In the barn there were only three bedrooms, not six like in the big house. The kids would have shared rooms, most likely with Jessamine having her own.

"How did it go with Benny?" Jessamine asked.

"We had a nice visit, but he seems really, really sick, Jess."

"Yeah," Jessamine agreed sadly. "But he'll get better soon."

"I hope so," Vivian agreed, purposely ignoring any innuendo on her friend's part. The last thing she wanted to do was dodge a romance with Giovanni's brother.

"It seems like you and Giovanni are friends," Jessamine said, and Vivian was caught off guard.

"I guess so," she stammered.

"I've been running interference for you because I didn't want things to be awkward," Jessamine said.

"I'm sorry," Vivian said.

"Don't be sorry. I'm relieved. Now we can do things as a group. And we can add Benny, when he's up to it."

All of a sudden Vivian felt a tidal wave of guilt. Suddenly omission felt like lying, and she didn't want to lie to Jessamine, not about something so important. "Jess, I need to tell you something..."

Jessamine turned questioningly in her direction, but before Vivian could speak, the door opened and Giovanni walked in. "Hey, can I crash the tour?" he asked.

He hadn't knowingly interrupted Vivian as she was about to confess, had he? "Sure, I was about to show her upstairs," Jessamine said. Her phone rang and she turned to answer it and then covered it and spoke to Giovanni and Vivian. "I need to take this. Go on without me."

With a smile, Giovanni gestured for Vivian to precede him up the stairs. "If you will look to your left, you will see the beam Moss ran into and knocked himself out on when he was three. Turning to your right, you will notice the door that Jessamine used as a means to pull out her first tooth. And this was my room." He opened a door and held it for Vivian, closing it behind her.

"How much time do you think we have?" he whispered, wagging his eyebrows suggestively.

"Not nearly enough," she said. She walked to the window and looked out. "How many of you shared this room?"

"Three. Joe and Benny had bunk beds, and my bed was over here." He walked to the far wall.

"It's so cozy," she said.

"It was a great place to grow up," he agreed. "By the way, I think my family loves you."

She beamed. "I like them, too."

"No, you don't understand. They don't like you, they *adore* you. I think Mom might be drawing up adoption papers. Did you mean what you said back there? Did you really have a crush on me in high school?"

She eased closer but still out of touching distance. "I memorized your schedule so I could glimpse you in the hall between classes."

"Why didn't you ever say anything?" he asked.

"You were so aloof," she said.

"That was to cover my total and complete awkwardness at the thought of a girl getting close to me," he said.

"So you're saying if I had approached you in high school and confessed my crush, you wouldn't have known what to do with me?" she asked.

"I barely know what to do with you now," he said.

She pulled out her phone and began texting.

"What are you doing?" he asked.

"I'm sending you a text, detailing exactly what to do with me now," she said and pressed send as Jessamine opened the door.

Jessamine opened the door and saw Vivian standing silently with her arms crossed while Giovanni was engrossed in reading a text. "Giovanni, you haven't been on your phone the whole time, have you? Rude."

"Millennials. Aren't they the worst?" Vivian said.

Giovanni put her in a headlock and rubbed his knuckle on her scalp. "I'm getting out of here. I need some air." He let Vivian go and left the room.

"What was that about?" Jessamine asked.

Vivian shrugged. "Men. Come on, I want to see the horses."

On Monday, Evan Kincaid was waiting for Vivian in her office. He slid a cup of coffee across her desk like a bribe. "I have a proposition for you."

"What's that?" Vivian asked. She hadn't seen him much the last few weeks. She had hoped that was because he had picked up on her "not interested" signals.

"I heard a rumor about you."

She sipped the coffee. "What rumor?"

"I heard you used to run cross country," he said.

Relieved, she smiled. "That was a lifetime ago, and I wasn't very good."

"Still, you're the only person I know here who runs. There's a half marathon coming up, and I was wondering if you want to do it with me."

She blinked. "Evan, it's been years since I ran consistently, and I've never run thirteen miles."

"It's not until the spring so we'd have months to train," he said. "Come on, Vivian. We're both pushing thirty. Don't you want to have some accomplishments under your belt?"

"Actually, I do. I've been working on a sort of bucket list and running a race is on there," she admitted.

"Perfect," he said, smiling.

"The thing is, Evan, and I don't know how to say this delicately, I'm not interested in romance. You seem to be at a crossroads right now, and I'm, well, let's say I'm not emotionally available."

"Okay, fair enough. I've been occasionally and halfheartedly hitting on you. But I genuinely want to do this marathon, and I genuinely don't want to do it alone. Will you please do it with me if I promise to keep things purely platonic?"

"I need to talk it over with…myself. Can I let you know?"

"Sure, talk it over with yourself and get back to me," he said. He was laughing at her, and rightly so. Keeping so many secrets was making her come off like a kook. But the more she thought about doing the marathon, the more she wanted to, even if it was with Evan. She wasn't sure how to broach the subject with Giovanni, though. Theirs wasn't a typical arrangement. Would he have a problem with her spending time with Evan?

Mondays were American food night at their house. Giovanni had embraced Vivian's theme nights with gusto, mostly because he hadn't tasted much food outside his mother's cooking. And probably because they still ate a fair share of his mother's cooking. On the nights when Vivian didn't feel like making something, she could always open the fridge and pull out a Mama Samperi special. But tonight she was making meatloaf and mashed potatoes, one of Giovanni's favorites.

"Hey, meatloaf night," Giovanni announced when he walked in.

"You might be the only man in America who gets excited about meatloaf," she said.

"I'm a man of simple tastes, Vivy," he said. He nibbled a carrot while he watched her work. "Seeing you in the kitchen makes me understand why people watch cooking shows."

"Because it's soothing?" she guessed.

"Because pretty woman plus good food equals everything that's right with the world," he said. "God bless America."

"Giovanni, you know Evan from work?"

"Tarp guy, the constructor of young minds?"

"That's the one. He wants me to train for a marathon with him."

He snorted a laugh. "Wow."

"Wow what?"

'That's an original way to go about hitting on someone."

"I don't think he was hitting on me," she said.

"I do, and he was. What gave him the idea that you run?"

"Because I used to run in high school," she said.

"You did? I didn't know that. I'm really going to have to find one of our old yearbooks at some point," he said.

"Anyway, so do you mind if I do it?"

"Do what?" he said.

"Are we having the same conversation? Do you mind if I train to run a half marathon with Evan?"

He set aside the remainder of his carrot, turned around, and walked out of the room.

"Where are you going?" she called.

He didn't answer, so she followed him to the living room where he sat holding a book he wasn't actually reading. "What are you doing?"

"I'm regrouping so I don't yell," he said.

"Why?"

"Because I promised myself if I ever got married, I wouldn't yell like my parents," he said.

"Your parents seem happy."

"Of course they're happy. They're very much in love," he yelled, slamming the book to the couch.

"You said you didn't want to yell," she yelled.

He took a breath and lowered his voice. "Of course I don't want to yell. No one wants to yell, but what else am I supposed to do in this situation?"

"What situation?"

"When my wife wants to go off with another man and run a marathon?"

"But it's only running. I told him I'm not interested in him and he agreed it would be a platonic venture."

"A platonic venture? Oh, well, I feel loads better since I know it's merely a *platonic venture.*"

"I don't understand why you're angry with me when I haven't done anything. I'm asking you if you mind if I do something, which means you're mad about a hypothetical," she said.

"Because it makes me mad that you don't understand why I'm mad," he said.

"I have no idea, so why don't you tell me instead of blowing up at me?" she said, hands on hips and breathing hard. While he was sitting, she was taller and she enjoyed the height advantage.

"Because you're mine, Vivian, okay? I don't know where this primal urge is coming from, but there it is. I think of you with another man, and I want to grab you up and carry you away and hide you so no men will ever lay eyes on you again. You are mine, and I am yours, and that is the end."

"Well, yeah," she agreed, deflated. She sat in his lap, but he was still too angry to touch her, so she took his hands in hers and kissed his palms.

"What do you mean, 'well, yeah,'" he said.

"I don't think you're hearing me that I don't want Evan, Giovanni. I want you; I'm crazy about you. And he knows I don't want him because I told him so. But running a race is on my bucket list, and it's something I've wanted to do for a while now. It's hard to train by yourself for something like that, and I would appreciate his help. I genuinely don't believe he has any designs on me, but if it means that much to you, I'll tell him no."

His anger fizzled. "You're crazy about me?"

"I thought that was fairly obvious by the way I've been blatantly throwing myself at you," she said.

"How was I to know you weren't naturally that affectionate with everyone?"

"There's 'affectionate' and then there's 'I could get arrested for this.' I reserve the second one for you."

"You have a bucket list?"

"Yes."

"Can I see it?"

"It's kind of boring," she said. "Eloping with a stranger was far more exciting than anything on my list."

He took a breath and let it out slowly. "If doing the marathon is important to you, and it's something you want to do, then I think you should do it."

"Really?" she said.

"Really," he said. "And in case you couldn't tell by my caveman display, I'm fairly crazy about you, too."

"Maybe we should get married," she said.

"Don't push me, woman, I need my space."

She cozied closer to him and slipped her arms around his neck. "How much space?"

"Why don't you show me something else you could get arrested for and I'll let you know," he said and kissed her.

When the kiss was finished, she pulled away. "Hey, I think we had our first fight," she said.

"Then let's get busy with our first makeup session," he said.

"Did anybody ever tell you that you have a one track mind?" she asked.

"Choo, choo," he said and kissed her again.

⚿

*L*ater that week Evan and Vivian began training for the half-marathon. It had been a long time since Vivian ran, and she was out of shape, so much that it pained her to breathe, let alone talk. Four days a week, she stumbled out of bed before it was light and drove to the park where she met Evan for their run.

"I could pick you up," Evan offered.

"No, thanks," Vivian said.

"You know, Vivian, you're kind of making me feel like a lecher with this standoffishness you have going on."

"It's not you, Evan; it's me. My life is complicated right now."

"I get complicated. Carrie and I are trying to make things work again, but it's hard to come back together after a separation. She's at her place and I'm at my place. Everything feels so distant."

"It's not normal to have two different houses, is it?" she mused.

"No, it's not," he agreed. "Anyway, are you ready to run?"

"Yes," she said, but she couldn't help groaning a little. Each day they added distance to their run. Right now they were at five miles, and Vivian could feel it in every muscle.

"Only eight miles to go and we'll be set," he said, smiling.

"Has anyone ever told you you're way too cheery in the morning?"

"Only my wife," he said. "Opposites attract, and all that."

Vivian had never thought about it before, but Giovanni was definitely an early morning person while she did better after eight. In most other ways, though, they were extremely compatible. Were they supposed to be opposites? Did it mean something was wrong with them if they weren't? They were both quiet, rational, introverted, and married to their routines. Should one of them be a fun-loving extrovert? She pushed it from her mind, deciding not to borrow trouble. They were happy, even with so many secrets. Maybe what worked for them wouldn't work for everyone.

While she ran, she distracted herself with thoughts of the upcoming Thanksgiving. She and Giovanni hadn't yet talked about it. She wasn't sure how to broach the subject. She wanted to spend the day with him, and she didn't care where. Either at her house or at her sister's house didn't matter, as long as they were together. She would even be willing to split the day in half so each family got equal time. But what did Giovanni want?

She wouldn't have to wait long to find out. The next day, her sister called and she sounded upset.

"Mom and Dad aren't coming."

"Who is this?" Vivian asked.

"Vivian, be serious," Annie said impatiently.

"Did you really expect them to come, Annie?" Vivian said.

"No, but I hoped. They want us to come there. Can you believe that? I mean, I have two small children and you get two days off school and they want us to travel ten hours to visit. Seriously, what is wrong with them?"

"That's a discussion for another day," Vivian said. Annie had been angry at their parents since they moved to North Carolina and she was forever trying to get Vivian on her side while Vivian, who hated confrontation, preferred to remain neutral.

"Anyway, can you bring sweet potatoes and some kind of dessert?" Annie said.

"Uh," Vivian stalled. She and Giovanni still hadn't talked about their plans.

"What do you mean 'uh'? Do you prefer to bring something else? Because everyone likes your sweet potatoes better than mine, not that I'm bitter."

"No, it's just that I'm not exactly sure what I'll be doing that day yet," Vivian said. An ominous silence greeted her for a long moment before Annie spoke.

"What do you mean you're not sure what you're doing that day? Do you have an alternate family I don't know about? Are you also planning to move to the coast and abandon me?" Annie asked.

"No, it's just that," Vivian paused to dab her forehead. She was actually sweating, but Annie often had that effect on her. She had always been intense, but since having children and becoming a stay-at-home Mom the intensity had nowhere else to go and often wound up being channeled into Vivian's life. "All right, sweet potatoes are fine."

"And a dessert," Annie reminded her.

"A dessert," Vivian dutifully repeated.

"What dessert will you be bringing?" Annie asked. "I don't want mine to clash with yours."

"I'll get back to you," Vivian said.

"Good," Annie said, sounding much cheerier than she had at the beginning of the conversation. "We'll have fun, even if our parents don't think enough of us to leave their precious ocean for a visit."

Vivian hung up as Giovanni walked through the door. "What's up?" he greeted her, taking in her wan expression.

"I was talking to my sister," she said.

"Ah," he said. After only a few short weeks of marriage, he had come to recognize the signs of sibling fatigue whenever Vivian mentioned Annie.

"We were talking about Thanksgiving," Vivian said, trying to sound nonchalant. Giovanni froze, his hand on the item he'd reached for from the refrigerator. "It's kind of a big deal for her that I'm there because our parents aren't coming and she feels abandoned." There. Now the ball was in his court and she hadn't made any presumptions about the day.

Giovanni sat, sighing as he did so. "I'm kind of relieved to hear that."

"You are?" Vivian asked.

"I am. You see, every year for Thanksgiving we go to my Grandma's house in Brooklyn, and when I say house, I mean two-bedroom apartment. Everyone goes. My parents take the spare bedroom and my brothers and sister and I sleep on the floor in the living room like we have since we were kids.

"Even Peaches and Joe?" Vivian asked.

"Even Peaches and Joe," Giovanni said. "It's miserably crowded and loud and exhausting, but it's also kind of a requirement and I haven't been able to find a way to get out of it," he said. "I've been trying to find a way to tell you."

In other words, she wasn't invited.

He scrutinized her face. "Are you upset?"

"Why should I be?" she asked.

Neither of them could articulate a reason.

CHAPTER 15

"Why are you taking a fork to bed?" Benny whispered.

"To jab Moss if he starts to snore," Jessamine said.

"I don't snore," Moss protested. "I selectively filter air through alternating nostrils. It's music, if you think about it."

"Make music tonight, and I will jab you," Jessamine threatened, albeit in a whisper. The apartment was so tiny they had to whisper or risk waking their grandmother who, more often than not, would emerge with a wooden spoon held aloft, promising to punish the noisemaker. She was a wonderful grandmother, loving and generous. She was also the most terrifying person under five feet any of them knew.

"Mom and Dad have six bedrooms and an empty guest barn. Why do we have to come here and hole up in one room like drug smugglers in a shipping container?" Moss whined.

"Nonna doesn't travel," Benny said.

"Nonna can haul herself to the wharfs at six in the morning for fresh fish every Friday, but can't set foot on an airplane?" Moss said.

"It is what it is," Benny said, his tone a combination of Zen resignation and exhaustion.

Giovanni lay quietly, letting the chatter of his siblings swirl around him while he experienced a bizarre sense of déjà vu. He had occupied the same square footage on his grandmother's floor every Thanksgiving eve for as long as he could remember. And for whatever reason the experience had always inspired him to ponder his future. Since his job had been prescribed since childhood, he usually thought about his future house, his future car, and his future wife. Now he had the house, he had the car, and, as of three months ago, he had the wife. Now when he tried to picture his future, he came up empty. What would his family say if they knew about Vivian? Could he really imagine her occupying the space beside him on Nonna's carpet? He missed her warm, soft presence next to his. After espousing a happy bachelorhood for nearly three decades, he could barely remember life without her. How had he spent his evenings without her beside him, each of them happily engrossed in reading? How had he eaten so many meals alone? Before, he would have said his aloneness had been a happy refuge from a large family. Now he saw it for what it had been: lonely.

A pair of feet whooshed by him and he sat up. His sister-in-law had left the room. "Is Peaches sick?" he asked.

Jessamine sat up. "Peaches is sick?"

Moss arose as well. "What's wrong with Peaches?"

Joe sat up. Only Benny remained silent and supine, having finally succumbed to malaria-ridden exhaustion. "She's fine," Joe said. "She needed a break for a minute."

"From us?" Moss asked, sounding like an overly sensitive little boy.

"Not you guys, exactly. Just everything. It can be overwhelming for an outsider," Joe said.

"Outsider?" Giovanni echoed. Peaches had been coming to Thanksgiving for as long as he could remember, long before she and Joe were married. He had always thought of her as part of the family; everyone had.

Joe sighed. "Nonna asked about kids."

"Oh, Joe," Jessamine said.

"So?" Moss said and Jessamine punched him.

"So it's a sensitive subject, and having Nonna poke at it didn't help matters," Joe said with a concerned glance toward the bathroom.

"But everyone knows Nonna doesn't have a filter," Moss said and for once Giovanni agreed with him. Their grandmother said the first thing that came to her mind and assumed that everything in their lives was her business. During the difficult developmental teenage years, she had alternated between telling them they were getting too fat or too thin, occasionally mixing up her advice by offering them homemade remedies for acne.

"I know, but it's different for Peaches," Joe said.

"Why?" Moss asked.

"It just is. Shh," Joe whispered as the bathroom door opened. They all lay hastily back down as Peaches re-entered the room. She lay back down, sniffling a little in a way that made Giovanni's heart wrench for his sweet sister-in-law.

If Peaches, who had been a part of their family for nearly two decades, could still be ruffled by Nonna's insensitive commentary, how would a newcomer fare? Vivian, for instance. How would his charming little wife handle the formidable Nonna's intrusive probing? Vivian was self-contained and valued her privacy. Could she ever really fit in with his family who lacked boundaries, asked probing questions, and delved their noses where they didn't belong?

He lay awake long after his siblings had fallen asleep, his mind as uncomfortable as the rest of him.

*

At home in Kentucky, Vivian was having a similarly difficult time of things. Her sister was one of those type-A, high-strung personalities who broke down at the slightest provocation, only her version of a breakdown involved becoming increasingly brittle with stress. Holidays had always been a trigger for her, even before she was responsible for hosting them. As a kid, she usually wound up in tears on Christmas morning, approximately one hour after the presents had been opened. Their dad had once joked you could set your watch by the inevitability of one of Annie's meltdowns. To compensate, Vivian had learned to set her emotions aside and maintain a stoic front. As adults, they were no different.

"How can you not be mad at them?" Annie asked as she stalked around her kitchen, lifting lids and stirring things. "I mean, they basically abandoned us to move to their beloved ocean."

"Annie, we're not kids anymore," Vivian reminded her.

"Okay, but how about when we were kids? What about college?"

"What about it?" Vivian asked, her hand tensing on the potato peeler.

"I could be doing a lot better things with the massive amount of money I send to cover my loan every month, and I'm sure you could, too," Annie said.

"That's not Mom and Dad's fault," Vivian said.

"Isn't it? They didn't help either one of us with school," Annie said.

"So? They weren't obligated to. That's not exactly in the parent contract."

"No, it's not. It's not written down anywhere that you help your kids once they leave the nest, but you know what, Vivian? Normal parents want to, at least I do. I would do anything for Gertrude and Bowden, would go to any lengths to help them get a leg up in the world. I actually *want* to be with my kids, to spend time with them on holidays. Why don't Mom and Dad?" She used the back of her hand to swipe furiously at her tears.

Vivian swallowed hard. Annie had a point. On the other hand, it wouldn't accomplish anything to get angry with her parents. Her relationship with them was tenuous enough to begin with. Adding bitterness and resentment wouldn't help anything. "It is what it is, Annie. At least we have each other," Vivian said.

Annie nodded and sniffled again. "But I'm telling you, wait until you get married and have kids. Then you'll understand how it feels to be abandoned and alone. What's going to happen on Grandparents' Day at Gert's school? Am I going to have to send a note telling them Gert's grandparents won't be coming because they prefer to spend their time with the Atlantic instead of their granddaughter?"

Her sister continued to rant, but Vivian tuned her out. When she got like this, it was best to let her spew. In a while, she would calm down and the subject would be dropped. Meanwhile, Vivian distracted herself with thoughts of Giovanni. How would he view her parents' disinterest in her life? His family was so involved; would he view it as a character flaw on her part? For the past three months she had been dying to tell Annie her secret, but it had never occurred to her to tell her parents. Wasn't that weird? Shouldn't she have wanted to call them first thing to tell them she eloped?

She tried to imagine herself telling her parents about Giovanni. What would their reaction be? "That's nice, Vivian. Bring him by when you come to visit next year." What would involved parents do? Rush home to meet him? Throw a fit over the months of exclusion? Was that what Giovanni's parents would do? Probably. Vivian had the feeling that if Giovanni's mother ever found out their secret, it wouldn't go down well, regardless of her feelings for Vivian. She also had the feeling that if her parents found out, they would find it as interesting as a weather report.

The doorbell rang, startling her out of her reverie and putting an end to Annie's rant.

"Get that, would you?" Annie asked and Vivian, too distracted by daydreams, didn't suspect what was about to happen. Even after she opened the door to a man, she didn't suspect. It wasn't until after he spoke and had been invited inside that she started to understand.

"Hi, I'm Herman," he said, smiling broadly. Vivian returned his smile, wondering what a door-to-door salesman was doing out on Thanksgiving.

"Hi," she said, her gaze dropping to his feet. Where was his product? What was he selling?

"I'm Rob's cousin," he continued.

"Oh, I'm so sorry, come in," Vivian said, moving aside to usher him in. She had no idea anyone else was coming for lunch. Why hadn't Annie told her? "Can I take your coat?"

"Thank you," Herman said as he shucked out of his coat. She realized, as she reached for it, that he was a small man, nearly as short as she. "You must be Vivian."

Startled, she tried to figure out how he knew her name. "Were you at the wedding, Herman?" she asked. Rob and Annie's wedding had been nearly seven years ago. It had been a busy day. Would he fault her for not remembering him?

"I was there," he said. "And you can call me Pee Wee. Everyone does." He smiled, and that was when the awful truth hit her. This was a fix up; her sister was trying to fix her up with yet another man, and on Thanksgiving, no less. Worse, now that he had stepped into the bright light of the entryway, she could see the silver threads sparkling through his hair. Her audible groan was stopped only by the arrival of her brother-in-law.

"I'd better go help Annie in the kitchen," Vivian said while the men greeted each other. Neither of them noticed her escape, but Annie noticed her arrival.

"Annie!" Vivian hissed.

Annie looked up with a too-innocent smile. "What?"

"Why is that man here?"

"He's Rob's cousin," Annie said.

"And that's the only reason he's here?" Vivian asked.

Annie sighed, "Vivian, come on. Men aren't going to magically appear before you if you're not willing to put in the work."

"He has liver spots on his hands," Vivian declared.

"Those aren't liver spots; he has a skin condition," Annie said.

"*Ew*," Vivian said, wrinkling her nose in disgust.

"It's not contagious," Annie said. "At least I don't think it is. Anyway, he's a good guy. Don't let a few benign growths stand in your way."

"He's old," Vivian said.

"He's experienced," Annie said. "Give him a chance. He's coming off a really nasty divorce."

"Well, this keeps getting better and better—an unnaturally short, old man with skin mumps and a recent, nasty marital breakup? Let me at him!"

"You could do worse," Annie said.

"Worse than Pee Wee Herman?" Vivian exclaimed.

"Keep your voice down. He's not deaf," Annie said.

"Are you sure? Because that's the only thing he's missing at this point. Unless you're about to tell me he's incontinent. Don't you dare tell me that or I won't be able to contain myself. I'll run right out there and rip his suspenders and sock garters right off," Vivian said.

"I don't understand why you're getting so upset. I would think you'd be pleased I'm thinking of you with all these men," Annie pouted.

"You would think that," Vivian said. Her sister was myopic when her mind was made up.

"I want to see you settled," Annie said.

"You want me to settle," Vivian argued.

"All I'm asking is that you keep an open mind and give him a chance," Annie said.

"No. Absolutely not. I will be polite to him because he's Rob's cousin and your guest, but I will not even hint at anything more, and if you do, I'm leaving," Vivian said.

Annie sighed and rolled her eyes. "You're so dramatic."

"Yeah, I'm the dramatic one," Vivian muttered.

To Vivian's relief, Annie didn't try to pawn her off on Pee Wee, or even hint at romance. Vivian wanted to believe it was because she had come to her senses, but the reality was that she was too busy playing hostess and mother for anything else. Bowden and Gertrude were a full time job, let alone preparing and serving an entire Thanksgiving meal. Vivian tried to help where she could, but Annie was particular about how things were done.

When the day was over, she should have been relieved to go home, but she wasn't.

"Hey, Annie, do you mind if I stay over?" she surprised them both by asking.

"Of course not," Annie replied. "Why, though? You never ask to stay over. In fact, when I offer, you act like I'm trying to hand you some sort of punishment."

"I don't feel like going home to an empty house," Vivian said honestly. The house felt emptier without Giovanni. She had even tried going to his house to stay, but it felt equally cavernous, if not more so.

"All right," Annie said but began eying Vivian with the same sort of concerned suspicion she'd used after Gatlinburg.

By the next morning, Vivian was more than ready to go home. She had barely slept all night, not only because of her niece's incessant snoring—really, was there some sort of tonsil trouble going on?—but also because she had spent a lot of time thinking about Giovanni and their unique situation.

It occurred to her in the wee hours of the morning, as Gertrude snuggled close and snuffled loudly, that her situation wasn't normal. Who doesn't spend Thanksgiving with her husband? For that matter, who doesn't tell anyone she's married? And, as long as she was on the topic of secrets, why did she keep so many of them from Giovanni? And how many was he keeping from her?

They needed to talk, to figure out where they were headed in their relationship, and to begin to think about going public. And it was past time for Vivian to confess her crushing debt load, even if it affected his decision about their future. *Would* it affect his decision about their future? How could it not? It wasn't his debt; it was hers. But if they stayed married, it would become his problem, too. He would be trapped as much as she was, would have to start watching his pennies to help pay off her money woes. What man would willingly want that? And then there was her family. She would have to tell him that her parents were now only peripheral to her life. Any other man probably wouldn't care, but for Giovanni family was everything. Would he find her freakish for her lack?

"Are you all right?" Annie asked for the third time as Vivian zoned out over coffee.

"I didn't sleep much last night. Have you considered a sleep study for Gert? Because between the snoring and the twitching, I can't imagine she's ever getting to a REM cycle."

Now Annie turned her worried glance to her daughter. That

hadn't been Vivian's intent, but she couldn't deny her relief. "Maybe I should call the doctor today," Annie said.

"It wouldn't hurt to check into it," Vivian said. She stood and kissed the top of her niece and nephew's heads. "Thanks for everything, guys. I'm heading home now."

"But you only had coffee," Annie said.

"I'm still stuffed from yesterday. And I need to do my run; it goes better if it's not on an empty stomach."

"Are you still running with that guy, Evan?" Now Annie's laser focus was back on Vivian.

"Yes, but we're only friends."

"Lots of relationships start out as friends," Annie said.

"He's in the midst of a nasty separation," Vivian said.

"So he's fair game," Annie said.

"Annie!"

"All I'm saying is options are limited these days. You have to take what you can get, and you're always telling me you want someone young. Well, there you go."

"There is absolutely nothing between me and Evan, I can assure you. We barely even talk when we run. Basically we're there to make sure the other person doesn't keel over or get mugged." She checked the space on her arm where a watch would have been, if she wore a watch. "Look at the time, I really have to scoot."

"Call me later," Annie called.

"I will. I want to hear what the doctor has to say about Gert." She didn't, but she wanted to be the sort of aunt who kept up on those things. Maybe if she practiced keeping track of what went on with her niece and nephew, she would start to want to know about things like doctor visits and growth chart milestones. She and Annie only had each other; she should care about the details of her sister's life as much as Annie cared about hers. Or maybe not that much. No one should care that much.

After her run with Evan, Vivian still had a lot of time to kill until Giovanni came home. She spent that time writing a detailed outline explaining why she and Giovanni needed to talk and how to go about it. She had just put the finishing touches on her missive when the door opened and Giovanni entered the kitchen.

She stood. He opened his arms, and suddenly she was in them with neither of them having any memory of taking a step.

"Did you miss me?" he asked.

"Not hardly. I was too busy trying to decide if the old man my sister tried to fix me up with had scabies. What about you? Did you miss me?"

"I was about five minutes from drawing your face on a pillow and talking to it. Otherwise, no."

She pressed her face to his chest. "You smell like airplane."

"It's a new cologne I'm trying. Also, we got stuck on the runway for two hours. Flying is fun," he said.

"You know what you need right now?" she asked.

"Yes," he said.

"A shower," she said.

"Oh."

"I have this new shower gel that's supposed to encourage relaxation, but it's probably going to require a demonstration."

"Oh?"

"Why don't you take your stuff upstairs and I'll meet you there in a minute," she suggested. When he was safely out of the kitchen, she gathered her outline, folded it, and stuffed it in a drawer. Tonight wasn't the night for a deep discussion, but soon. She would broach all the issues between them as soon as the time was right.

CHAPTER 16

Giovanni and Vivian were both unusually excited about Christmas. For Vivian it marked two weeks off from school. For Giovanni, it marked the beginning of the slow season for business. They still worked some indoor renovation jobs, but it was nothing compared to the hectic building schedule of the warmer months.

"We're not going to leave this house or even this bed for three days," Giovanni vowed a week before Vivian's break began. "Maybe four days, depending on how long it takes bedsores to develop. You're a research whiz, look into it."

Vivian grunted in reply. Giovanni was always more awake and ready for conversation than she was in the morning, especially on Saturdays when he woke at six for work. The next time she opened her eyes, it was after eight and Giovanni was long gone. She rose and went to the park where she met Evan for a lengthy, exhausting run. While she was finishing her post-run shower, her sister called.

"They're coming!" Annie announced excitedly.

"Aliens?" Vivian guessed.

"Mom and Dad. They're coming for Christmas. I laid the guilt on pretty thick, but it worked and they're coming."

"Great," Vivian said. She had planned to mail their presents and was delighted at the postage she'd save.

"Of course they'll have to stay with you," Annie continued.

"Wait, what?"

"I don't have an extra guest room, and you have two of them. What's the big deal?" Annie asked. "It's not like you've ever been messy a day in your life, so there shouldn't be much cleaning involved. And I'm planning to handle most of the meals over here, so you won't have to spend the whole time cooking. Basically you'll be like a hotel, only free. Just make sure you have the good coffee Dad likes. You know how he gets without his coffee."

Annie prattled a while longer as Vivian made appropriate noises of agreement, but what else could she say? *Mom and Dad can't stay with me because where will my secret husband go?*

She must have sat at the table for a long time after the phone call with Annie because she was still there when Giovanni arrived.

"What's wrong?" he asked. "You look the same as you did that time you ate too much scampi."

"My parents are coming for Christmas," she said. "And they're staying here."

"Oh." He sat down heavily in the chair beside her.

"They haven't been here on a holiday in four years, so it's kind of a big deal."

"Oh," he said again.

"I'm not all that close to them," she blurted before she could lose courage.

"I picked up on that," Giovanni said.

"It's not that I don't love them or that they don't love me. It's just that they had us when they were really young. I guess they wanted to sew some wild oats. I left for college, and three weeks later the house was sold and they moved away."

"That must have been hard," Giovanni said.

"I've always been independent, and it was one of their favorite things about me," Vivian said. "For holidays, I went to Annie's. I spent my summers with my parents because being in a tourist town is a great place to get a job when you're a college kid, but it never felt like home. It's not that they're bad people," she hastened to add. "They were great when we were growing up. I think they felt like as soon as we were out of the house, they were done."

"Parents never stop being parents, or so my mother had tattooed on her bicep," he said.

Vivian laughed, but it turned into a sniffle. "You must think I'm a crybaby," she said.

"You've cried twice since I've known you," he said.

"I bet Jessamine never cried like this," Vivian said.

"Jess has also cried twice since I've known her, but she's dead inside, so I'm not sure I'd make her your role model."

"Things have been so sketchy with my parents the last few years; I want this visit to be perfect," she said.

"It will be," he promised. "We'll make it work. I'll stay at my house and we'll text a lot, like we're two teenagers who have been grounded. We'll be like Romeo and Juliet, plus cell phones, minus all the poison."

"That's going to depend on whether or not my sister tries to set me up with another geriatric lothario. If I see one more hopeful old man sitting at my holiday table, I'm going to pop a cyanide capsule. Hopefully with my parents here she'll be content to try and micromanage their lives instead of mine."

"When are they coming?" Giovanni asked.

"Three days," Vivian said.

"That doesn't leave us much time," Giovanni said.

"No, it doesn't," Vivian agreed.

"Maybe I should give you your present now."

"You bought me a present?" she asked. It was a stupid question, considering the holiday, but their relationship was so atypical that she hadn't been sure what to expect. And it was an intimate thing to buy a man a gift. She had struggled for weeks over what to buy him and had secretly been selling some of her old books to a used bookstore to afford a nice book for him. It was all very O. Henry.

"Be right back," Giovanni said in the excited tone of a four year old about to present his mother with his newest drawing.

Vivian waited nervously at the table. He returned a minute later with a beautifully wrapped tiny box. Her heart thrummed as she opened it and came face to face with a platinum wedding band.

"I didn't want to pick out a diamond without your input, so I thought this would be a good compromise," he said.

"I love it," she said, and she did. There was delicate filigree on the outside, giving it a vintage appearance. It was exactly what she would have chosen for herself, but she was confused. A ring was a symbol of marriage, one for everyone to see. Was he telling her he was ready to go public? She hoped so, but before she could ask, he answered by handing her a delicate gold chain.

"I hope this is the right length," he said.

"I'm sure it will be fine," she said, trying hard to hide her disappointment. She had a ring now, an actual token of their marriage. No longer could her mind try to convince her it had all been a dream. Even if she didn't wear it on her finger, she could still wear it. "You know, Giovanni, I'm not usually materialistic, but this ring means you are now officially my favorite husband."

"For the record, how many more husbands are you planning to acquire?" he asked.

"It depends on how many more gems my sister lobs my way. You know I can't resist a man with dentures," she said.

He pulled her into his lap. "Can you resist a man without dentures?"

"It's not just the dentures—you're also missing the rheumatism and glaucoma, but I'll try."

"Do your best," Giovanni said.

"Oh, I will," Vivian promised, and then she kissed him.

Three days later, her parents were there and all traces of Giovanni had been expunged. Somehow the house even smelled empty without him. She was wheeling one of her mother's suitcases inside when her sister called.

"Are they there? What are you doing now?"

"Why don't you come over?" Vivian suggested. "We'll have some cookies and cocoa."

"It's the kids' bedtime," Annie said.

"They can stay up late for one night," Vivian said.

"I suppose," Annie said. "Be there in a minute."

She must have tossed the kids in the car and sped because she arrived less than ten minutes later. The kids were shy around the grandparents they barely remembered. Bowden clung to Annie's leg and Gert peered out from behind Vivian. Vivian picked her up and brought her closer to her mother.

"Look, Gert, your hair is the same color as Grandma's," she said.

"So is yours," Gertrude said.

"That's because we're family," Vivian said.

"Mom's is yellow," Gertrude pointed out.

"That's because she's adopted," Vivian said.

"Vivian," Annie exclaimed. "Don't tell her stuff like that. She's literal; she'll believe you."

Their dad laughed. "I see you still enjoy being teased as much as ever, Annie Lou." He reached out and took Gert from Vivian. "My hair used to be yellow before it turned white."

"Will Mom's hair turn white?" Vivian asked.

"Not if L'Oréal has anything to say about it," Vivian remarked, earning another frown from her sister.

"So, what's been going on with you girls?" their mother asked.

"Didn't Vivian tell you her big news?" Annie asked.

"What big news?" her mom asked.

"Tell them, Vivian," Annie commanded.

"Um," Vivian stalled. Surely her sister couldn't be thinking what she thought she was thinking, could she?

Annie sighed impatiently. "A giant tree fell on Vivian's bedroom. She could have died." She flung it out like an accusation, as if it had been her parents' fault that the decrepit tree had decided to commit hara-kiri on Vivian's abode.

"Goodness," her mom said while her dad's gaze panned the room.

"I don't see a hole now," he said.

"The Samperis fixed it," Vivian said.

"The Samperis? What did you do, rob a bank? I didn't think they took on small jobs," he said.

"Their daughter, Jessamine, is a friend of mine," Vivian said.

"Looks like they did a good job," her father said.

"They did," Vivian agreed. "They even managed to match the roof tiles perfectly."

"It's like nothing ever happened," her mother said.

Vivian couldn't agree because, while the house looked the same, everything in her life was different now.

Annie sighed, bringing Vivian to the realization that there was an undercurrent of tension in the room. Either Vivian could try to diffuse it or Annie would erupt again.

"Who wants to help me make cookies?" she asked.

"I do," Gert volunteered, shooting her hand into the air like a model pupil.

"Awesome. How about Grandma, should she help us?" Vivian asked.

"I'd love to," her mother said.

"Dad, Bowden loves to read, and I brought home a whole stack of picture books from the library. They're right there," Vivian said, pointing to a neatly stacked pile in the corner.

"You keep picture books at your work? What kind of high school are you running there?" her dad joked.

"I went to the public library," Vivian said.

"Scouting out the competition, eh?" he said, but he settled Bowden in his lap and picked up a book.

Annie plopped into a chair, scowling. Vivian could almost read her mind. She wanted to find something to be angry about because she wasn't ready to let go of her resentment yet. But Vivian didn't like confrontation and arguing, and this was her house. As long as they were here, they were all going to get along.

And they did. They baked cookies, drank cocoa, snacked, and talked until the kids began to rub their eyes and whine.

"I've got to get these two home before the meltdowns begin," Annie said. Vivian was pleased to hear the regret in her tone. It had been a fun, carefree evening. She only hoped they could keep it going through the remainder of Christmas. All they had to do was keep things light and fun; for her part that meant no bombshell announcements about clandestine elopements. For the first time since her hasty marriage to Giovanni, she was glad they were keeping everything a secret.

CHAPTER 17

Since he last saw Vivian, Giovanni had barely left his family. Without her, his house felt cavernous. In an astonishingly short amount of time, he had formed a Vivian-shaped hole and nothing else could fill the void. Before when he pictured the sort of woman he'd end up with, she had looked nothing like Vivian. The former woman of his dreams would have been a tall, cool blonde, a venerable ice queen. Now that he was married to a soft, warm little librarian, he couldn't believe he had ever wanted anything else. No doubt about it, he and Vivian fit together in a way he couldn't articulate. Was she perfect? No. Did she do things that annoyed him? Yes. Would he trade her for anyone? Definitely not.

And now he was without her for days on end, left with only his family to fill the vacuum.

"Why are you here?" Moss asked.

"What are you talking about?" Giovanni asked.

"You usually stay away until the last possible minute, until supper is literally on the table, and then Mom has to call and command you to come over. And now you're here every day. Is there something you're not telling us? Is it me? Am I dying?" Moss began to pat his body, as if he could feel the hidden malignancy.

"Yes, Moss, you're dying. That's why we've all gathered here at Mom and Dad's house. Way to ruin the secret. Try to act surprised on Christmas morning when we tell you," Giovanni said.

"Someday it's going to happen, and won't you feel bad," Moss said.

"We'll see," Giovanni replied

"So what are you doing here?" Moss asked.

"Benny's home," Giovanni evaded. "I haven't seen him in a long time."

It didn't matter how he answered because Moss was no longer paying attention. Birdlike, he had caught sight of his reflection in a window and was now tousling his fingers through his hair.

"When are you going to get a haircut?" Giovanni asked.

"Never. I'm like Samson; my hair is my strength," Moss said as one of his unruly curls tumbled into his eyes.

"You're more like a salmon—googly-eyed and easily picked off by a hungry bear," Giovanni said.

"The ladies love Moss," Moss said.

"Mom doesn't count," Giovanni informed him.

Jessamine arrived with a giant leather bag slung over her arm.

"New purse?" Giovanni asked.

"Since when do you notice my purses?" Jessamine said.

He hadn't noticed her purse so much as he had suddenly realized the lack of Vivian's purses. She always used the same sensible cross-body bag. Was that because she didn't like purses? While he was on the subject, he inspected his sister's shoes. Those looked new, too. Vivian hadn't bought new shoes since he'd known her. In fact, she hadn't bought anything for herself. Was she one of those rare people who didn't like to shop?

"Giovanni is being weird today," Moss informed her.

"Just today?" Jessamine said. "So, who all is coming this year?" She set her bag aside and sat down.

"Everyone," Moss said.

It was the day before the day before Christmas and also time for their family's annual company party. They invited all the contractors they worked with throughout the year; the plumbers, excavators,

HVAC specialists and anyone else they occasionally called in for a project. As Moss said, everyone came to the party. It had become almost legendary, mostly because of their mother's food. Although she hired a couple of college kids to serve as waiters, Mama Samperi insisted on preparing the food herself, from *insalata* to *biscottos*, everything was made from scratch. The only thing she purchased was the gelato, and that was only because she found a supplier who was a distant cousin and made it from an authentic Italian recipe.

"Molly's here," their father boomed from the entryway.

"Oy," Moss said, and scurried away.

Molly, the company's secretary and only fulltime non-family employee, had entertained a not-so-secret crush on Moss for the past three years. Everyone but Moss thought she could do better.

"Merry Christmas," Molly said as she approached.

"Merry Christmas," Benny answered as he also joined their group.

"Molly, you look beautiful. Is that a new dress?" Jessamine asked.

"Kind of," Molly said and gave a self-conscious tug to the dress.

"Do women buy new clothes and bags and shoes a lot?" Giovanni asked.

"Only when we're breathing," Jessamine said. She made no secret of the fact that she loved to shop. What most people didn't realize was that she also made a lot of money by reselling things. Previously, she had tossed around the idea of opening a consignment boutique on the side but lacked the time and energy such a large venture would require.

"Not all women are into material things," Benny inserted and Jessamine rolled her eyes.

"You're presuming that wanting to have nice things equates with being shallow," Jessamine argued.

"I'm not presuming anything. I'm simply saying that not all women are into keeping up on the latest fashion," Benny said.

"What do you think, Molly?" Giovanni asked. His siblings would take opposing viewpoints and argue them for sport. He wanted an objective opinion.

"Most women I've known enjoy having new things, but 'new' is a relative term. For some people, having something new means buying designer items while some other people might prefer scouring for treasures at a thrift store. Personal preference, I guess," Molly said.

Giovanni nodded, thinking. Vivian did neither of those things. Except for groceries and toiletries, she hadn't shopped once since he'd known her. But before he could spend too much time wondering over her shopping habits, an influx of people arrived and the party officially began.

⚷

Vivian had just removed her sweater when she received a text from Giovanni.

What are you doing?

Smiling, she replied:

Getting ready for bed. What about you?

Open the window and find out, he replied.

She turned to the window and nearly yelped when she saw him outside. She pushed open the window, praying it wouldn't squeak.

"What are you doing?" she asked.

"I couldn't not see you on Christmas," he said as he pitched forward and began hauling himself inside.

"It's Christmas Eve," she told him and reached out to give him a hand.

"Close enough," he said.

She braced her feet and yanked as he gave a final push off the ladder. With so much momentum, they toppled onto the floor with an echoing thump. Vivian closed her eyes and held her breath, waiting for one of her parents to run into the room to check on her. They had to have heard the noise. In fact, half the neighborhood had probably heard the noise.

"Are you all right?" Giovanni asked.

She nodded. "What if someone sees the ladder? They might think it was a burglar and call the police."

"If someone is out at midnight on Christmas Eve inspecting your windows, I'd be more concerned about them," Giovanni said. "Besides, the streets were almost completely deserted on the way over here. I think we're safe." He sat up a little, enough for her to finally draw a deep breath. "Hey." He smiled.

"Hey," she said, smiling in return. "Merry Christmas."

"Merry Christmas. How did it go with your family tonight?" He stood, scooped her onto the bed, stripped down to his underwear, and slid in beside her.

"Annie only had one meltdown and she didn't spring any more geezers on me. The kids are starting to warm up to my parents, and my parents seem to be having fun with the kids. All in all it couldn't have gone any better. How was your night?"

"Loud," Giovanni said. The space between his brows puckered slightly.

"Did something happen?" she asked.

"I think something might be wrong with Peaches. She seems so sad lately, and she and Joe…there's a distance," he said.

"What do you think the problem is?" Vivian asked.

"I don't know. At Thanksgiving, Joe mentioned something about the family being too much for her sometimes." He sifted his hand gently through her hair, letting the velvety strands cascade through his fingers like a waterfall. Would his family be too much for Vivian? It was a heavy thought, one that nagged constantly at the back of his mind. Would Joe someday have to choose between Peaches and the family? It was too much for Giovanni to contemplate.

Meanwhile Vivian was thinking about her family. Which was worse, too much involvement or not enough? There had to be a happy medium somewhere.

For the next two hours they talked almost nonstop, about their families, about books they were reading, and about nothing at all. Vivian's eyes were drowsy with sleep, but she had never felt happier. A disproportionate amount of their relationship so far had been physical, so much that she sometimes wondered if that was all that was between them. But now they hadn't seen each other for days and all they were doing was talking.

"Giovanni," she whispered after a moment of silence.

"Hmm," he said. His eyes were closed.

"We've been lying next to each other in our underwear for hours and you haven't tried anything on me," she said.

"Wha'sis your point, Vivy?" he slurred sleepily.

"Maybe we're not newlyweds anymore. Maybe it's all downhill from here," she said.

"Are you trying to trick me into proving there are plenty more hills to climb?" he asked.

"Yes."

"Good," he said. Now fully awake, he reached for her.

A few hours later, Giovanni woke Vivian to kiss her goodbye. She didn't want him to go and kept up a string of conversation to prolong him. Both of them forgot to whisper. Soon a loud knock sounded on Vivian's door, and they froze.

Busted, Vivian thought. It was one of her parents, and they'd been caught. They would ask about the noise, and then they would see Giovanni. Everything would be out in the open. She couldn't possibly be more relieved. But she didn't want Giovanni to guess her relief, so she rolled out of bed with a worried frown and tiptoed to the door.

"Yes?" she said, opening the door a crack.

"Sorry to disturb you, Vivian," her dad said. "But I can't find the new coffee."

"You can't find the new coffee," Vivian repeated dumbly.

"I know you said you bought some, but I can't find it," he said.

"And that's why you're knocking on my door, because you can't find the coffee," she said.

"You did buy it, right? Because Mom is making breakfast, and I know we'll all want coffee. I can't imagine any store is open on Christmas morning."

"It's in the cupboard to the left of the sink. It probably got shoved behind the toaster after we used it yesterday," Vivian said.

"Oh, all right, thanks. Go back to sleep, if you want. Mom says breakfast won't be ready for about an hour," her dad said.

"Thanks," Vivian said. The hint of sarcasm in her tone was lost on him. She closed the door and turned back to the bed. Giovanni was lying in plain sight. If her dad had looked into her room even a little, he would have seen him. She crawled back into bed. "I'm going to build a time machine, go back to high school, and see how much stuff I could get away with. I thought my parents' total self-absorption was a new thing, but maybe not. Maybe they've always been in their own world and I never realized."

"If you go back to high school, look me up and put the moves on me," he said.

"As adult me or as high school me?" she said.

"Both," he said. He sat up and gave her a kiss. "I should go before someone notices the ladder."

"It won't be my parents," she assured him. "You could probably walk naked through the living room and they wouldn't notice."

"Tempting as that is, I think I'll use the ladder," he said. "I'll see you in two days."

"Two long days," she said gloomily.

He dressed hastily, opened the window, and slipped onto the ladder. "Hey, Vivian."

"What?" she was sitting up, watching him with a mellow sort of sadness.

"Your parents may not notice every detail of your life, but they do love you," he assured her.

"I know," she said.

"And what they lack in noticing about you, I more than make up for because, believe me, you are in my spotlight."

"Back at you," she said, smiling. She threw him a kiss. He pretended to catch it before disappearing down the ladder.

For the past two New Year's Eves, Jessamine had invited some members of the book club to her house for a party. This year was no exception. Vivian couldn't think of a polite refusal, but all she really wanted to do was stay home and celebrate with Giovanni.

"What do you usually do?" she asked, secretly hoping he would ask her to stay home and be with him.

"Something with the family," he said. "Mom makes a big production with lots of food."

"How are you not five hundred pounds?" she wondered, and not for the first time.

"I work with my hands," he explained, holding them aloft for her inspection.

"And what fine hands they are," she said, kissing them. "Maybe when we get home we can pretend it's midnight all over again and have our own celebration. You know they say the person you kiss at midnight will be the person you spend the next year with."

"Sounds good," he said and resumed reading his book. Vivian picked up her book, trying not to be disappointed in his lackluster attitude. She was tired of spending their holidays apart, but clearly it didn't bother him.

"By the way," he added in the same casual tone, "I don't ever want to be apart from you on Christmas like that again. There were a few days there when I genuinely thought I might die from loneliness and boredom."

"So you did miss me."

"Only in the way you might miss an arm or a leg," he said, setting aside his book and wrapping his arms around her.

Let's stay here, she wanted to say, burying her face in his neck. But he checked his watch and sat up. "I should go or my mom will send out the hounds." He kissed her. "Remember, you and me, fake midnight tonight."

"I won't forget," she said. "Have fun."

"You too," he said before grabbing his keys and dashing out the door.

With time to kill, Vivian put extra care into her appearance. Her hair was long and thick and she didn't always have time or energy to style it, but tonight she did, using her straightener to get perfect waves all around her head. With some surprise, she noted the pleasant changes in her body. Since she had started to train for the marathon, she was more toned. Her curves were in all the right places and she had dropped a few pounds. She fished into the back of her closet for the little black dress she hadn't been able to wear since college. Makeup wasn't her specialty so she watched a YouTube tutorial and tried to emulate a smoky effect on her eyes. It wasn't perfect, but it was a step up from her usual smattering of shadow and mascara.

"Not bad, Vivian," she admitted as she inspected herself in the mirror. Usually when she went out with Jessamine and Vivica, she didn't try because what was the point? But tonight she almost felt like she could hold her own with her two beautiful friends. Maybe it was the effect of being loved so well by a good man. Giovanni was making happiness beams shoot out of her, and she had no one to tell. She sighed and pushed the thought away, determined not to let anything spoil her good mood. She would have a pleasant night with her girlfriends and, later, she and Giovanni would celebrate. Privately. Where no one would ever see or know.

Sighing again, she grabbed her keys and drove to Jessamine's. The YouTube tutorial had pushed her into overtime so that she was a few minutes late getting to her friend's house. There were several cars in the lot, more than usual. Jessamine answered the door with a hug before shoving a party hat into Vivian's hands.

"Vivian, you look amazing," Jessamine whispered.

"Thanks," Vivian said, suddenly self-conscious. She smoothed an imaginary wrinkle from her dress.

Jessamine leaned closer and whispered. "Benny's here. It's almost like you knew."

"Oh," Vivian drawled. "I, uh…"

"Don't go shy on me. Come on." She grabbed Jessamine's hand and led her to the kitchen where she saw Benny, flanked by Moss and Giovanni. "You remember my brothers, Benny, Moss, and Giovanni." She flicked a dismissive hand in Giovanni's direction.

"Vivian!" Moss exclaimed, and picked her up.

"Set her down, Moss, she's not a stuffed animal," Giovanni said.

"Sister Vivian," Benny said. "I was beginning to think of you as my imaginary friend. It's good to see you in 3D."

"I'm glad to see you looking a little better," Vivian noted. His color was returning to normal and his sunken features had begun to fill out.

"It would be hard to look any worse," he said.

"Vivian, you're looking well," Giovanni said. "Is that a new dress?" Surely someone else had to notice the way he was looking at her, like he wanted to eat her on a cracker.

Vivian looked down to break eye contact before she did something she'd regret. "No, it's old. I've had it since college. It's weird, but I haven't shopped in months."

"Sounds like you need to get out more," he said.

"Some days it feels like I'm being held prisoner," she replied.

"Is it prison if you're a willing captive?" he mused.

"What are you talking about?" Jessamine asked him.

"I was being philosophical," Giovanni said.

"Stop it, it's weird," Jessamine said. "But Vivian, you seriously look spectacular. I think you've lost weight."

Vivian tugged self-consciously on her dress again. "Maybe a little. I've been training for a marathon."

Benny whistled. "A marathon, that's impressive."

"*Half* marathon," Vivian corrected. "Not that impressive."

"Still impressive," Giovanni said. "Thirteen miles is thirteen miles more than any of us have ever run."

"Unless Ma is chasing us with a spoon," Moss interjected.

"You'd think he's joking, but no," Benny said. "Don't tell the PC police, but we were spanked."

"Not nearly as often as we deserved," Jessamine added.

"Speak for yourself," Moss replied, rubbing his backside. "I'm still in pain."

"That's because you probably got paddled this morning," Jessamine said.

"Who told?" Moss asked.

"Can I get you something to drink, Vivian?" Giovanni asked.

"Yes, please. I brought cookies," she said, handing a plate to Jessamine.

"You cook?" Giovanni asked.

"Sometimes. And sometimes I open the fridge and eat whatever is there," Vivian said.

"Sounds like a good life," he said.

"I have no complaints," she agreed.

"What's in the cookies?" he asked.

"Chocolate, what else?" she said.

"You never know. You can't be too careful with baked goods. I'm partial to brownies, myself."

"Really? I know a guy at the farmer's market who makes the best. He puts a little something extra in them," Vivian said.

"I feel like I've had those before," Giovanni said.

"Wait, are you talking about those brownies you had tested at the lab?" Moss asked.

"You had brownies tested at a lab?" Vivian asked.

"Uh…" Giovanni stammered.

"Yeah, get this. Giovanni comes to me and asks if I know any labs that test for pot in brownies. He thought he got dosed with something at a party or something. You don't know Giovanni well, but he's like the last person who would ever eat pot brownies. It was pretty funny. Especially when they came up negative like, really, Giovanni, nice try attempting to be wild, but no," Moss said.

"So the brownies were fine?" Vivian asked.

Giovanni gave her a sheepish smile. "It turns out that any crazy behavior on my part had nothing to do with anything I ate," he said.

"What crazy behavior?" Jessamine asked.

"I sang karaoke," Giovanni said.

"What? No way," Benny said.

"Video or it didn't happen," Moss said.

"You know, I have a karaoke machine," Jessamine said.

"Let's go pick out something humiliating for him to sing," Moss said and left the kitchen, Benny and Jessamine trailing in his wake.

"You had the brownies tested," Vivian said. "Were you ever going to tell me?"

"I was saving it for our anniversary," Giovanni said. He put his hand on her hip and pulled her closer.

"I thought you were going to your parents," she said.

"And not be with my wife on New Year's Eve? What kind of monster do you think I am?" he asked.

"You're enjoying all of this a little too much," Vivian said.

"I would be enjoying it more if it were you and me on the couch, minus all the other people," he said. "And clothes. Although this dress is speaking my language."

"I don't see a way we could both reasonably sneak out now," she said.

"We'll have to make the best of it," he said. His other hand rested on her other hip and her arms snaked around his neck. Someone could come into the kitchen at any time, and Vivian couldn't care less. In fact, she hoped someone did. Giovanni seemed equally untroubled as he stood searching her face. Was he weighing the pros and cons of letting the cat out of the bag?

"Did I tell you that you look beautiful?" he asked.

"Don't get used to it; it was a lot of work to put this all together," she said.

"*Sei sempre bella*," he said.

"If you continue to speak Italian to me, I will swoon right here," she warned him.

"Maybe I'd better save it for later," he said.

"Unless you want to peel me off the floor, it's probably a good idea. Are you going to translate what you just said for me?" she asked.

"I'll save that for later, too," he said and kissed her. A loud exclamation from the other room startled them apart.

"Do I look like someone who has been kissed into oblivion?" Vivian asked, touching her fingers to her puffy lips.

"A little," he admitted. "Do I?"

"Not nearly enough," she said. "How do you manage to look unruffled all the time?"

"I'm melting on the inside," he said, placing his hand over his heart.

Vivian didn't want to leave the cozy circle they had created in the kitchen, but neither did she want to be rude to Jessamine. "I guess we should go out one at a time. You first so I can ice my lips."

"There's a back door to this place. Are you sure you don't want to escape, go home, and wear fewer clothes?"

"I'm only wearing a dress," she said.

"Exactly."

She smiled. "I'd love to, but I don't want to hurt your sister's feelings. You go, I'll be out in a minute." She gave him a gentle shove toward the door and turned her back on him to dig in her purse. She had a mirror and lip gloss in there somewhere, but it was undoubtedly at the bottom.

When she felt presentable again, she went into the living room and saw that Vivica had arrived and was standing beside Giovanni, her arm tucked into his elbow as she stared up at him with a flirtatious expression.

So this is what jealousy feels like, Vivian thought. Her gut felt like she had swallowed a capsule of glass shards. She had always eschewed such paltry emotions as a waste of energy, born of insecurity and immaturity. And though she didn't consider herself immature, she was the first to admit she was insecure in her relationship with Giovanni. True, they were married and things had been going well. But no one knew they were married, including Vivica who had doubtless heard of Giovanni's earlier interest in her.

Vivian forced aside her impulse to sprint across the room, pry Vivica's fingers off of Giovanni, and shout, "Mine, mine, mine!" Vivica had no idea Giovanni was taken. And, on closer inspection, Giovanni wasn't exactly responding warmly to Vivica's touch. He seemed distracted and uncomfortable. She took a breath and continued into the room like a grownup who was fully in charge of her faculties and not like an escapee from a teenage melodrama.

She sat on the couch and smiled at the people already mid-conversation. She had no idea what they were talking about, but she nodded pleasantly as if she were listening. But inside, she was going down a dark path. Did Vivica's arrival remind Giovanni that he had wanted her first? That Vivian had been the unwanted mistake? Did he still feel that way? Attempts to push that thought away repeatedly failed. How could someone not prefer Vivica to her? Even from across the room, Vivica shimmered. It was like being near a Hollywood actress in real life. She had claimed all the male attention in the room in one way or another. Moss was practically drooling and even Benedict, who seemed like he would be above such things, was secretly darting glances in her direction. Two of Jessamine's male friends, Jeremy and Carson, weren't even pretending not to drool over her.

"I noticed you forgot your drink," Giovanni spoke, bringing Vivian's attention back to the present. He stood before her, cup in hand.

"Thank you," she said, reaching for it. He smiled as he handed it over and then sat on the floor beside her, his back resting against the couch near her legs. Vivian wanted to reach out and touch him, but Jessamine was watching them curiously.

"It's game time," Jessamine announced amidst a round of groans. "Hey, you knew what you were getting into when you accepted the invitation. It's game night, people."

Vivian clapped.

"See? Vivian's excited," Jessamine said.

"Vivian's never played with this many Samperis before," Jessamine's longtime friend, Carolyn, said. "It's going to be a bloodbath, Vivian."

"We'll see," Vivian said. She knew from playing games with Giovanni and Jessamine that the Samperis were extremely competitive. She also knew she was equally competitive, if not more so.

"I think it should be guys against girls," Jessamine said.

"No way," Giovanni declared.

"Why?" Benny asked.

"Because Vivian's a librarian. She knows things," Giovanni said. He tapped his temple.

"She may know some things, but all women have the same Achilles heel named sports," Moss said.

"And you're not married why, Moss?" Carolyn asked, mussing his hair.

"I'm saving myself for someone special," Moss said, batting her hand away.

"You're saving yourself for someone who babies you as much as your mom does," Carolyn said.

"That too," Moss agreed. "I agree with Jess, guys against girls. Let's wipe the floor with them quickly and move on with our lives, gentlemen."

Benny put up his hands. "I am having no part of that statement."

"Don't say I didn't warn you," Giovanni said.

"Are you sc-sc-scared?" Moss asked him.

"Yes," Giovanni said.

Later, after the game of trivia was finished and the women had wiped the floor with the men, Giovanni said, "I tried to warn you."

"How could you possibly know that Vivian was going to go Jean Grey from the X-men and destroy us all?" Moss asked.

"Look at her, she looks like a killer," Giovanni said. He squeezed her knee in the spot he knew she was ticklish and she dove forward to shove his hand away.

"She looks like one of those Beanie Babies you used to get with a Happy Meal," Moss said.

"I don't think I like either of those descriptors," Vivian said.

"The point is we won and you lost," Vivica said. "And now everyone knows it's always best to have a reference librarian on your side."

"The final exam for my degree was one massive game of *Jeopardy*," Vivian said.

"Really?" Moss asked and Jessamine smacked him upside the head.

"No, not really, Moss. Use your brain."

"My brain is tired from trivia," Moss said.

"You answered one question," Benny said.

"And you got it wrong," Giovanni added.

"But the point is that I provided moral support and team spirit," Moss said. "And now I suggest we play a man's game."

"Go-on-a-date-and-never-call-again Monopoly?" Vivica said.

"Leave-the-toilet-seat-up Roulette?" Jessamine added.

"A rousing edition of How-to-avoid-a-relationship Candyland?" Carolyn suggested.

"I'm feeling a lot of bitterness in this room," Moss said. "Anything you want to add, Vivian?"

"I have no complaints," Vivian said.

"Hmm, let's see how you feel after we beat you at poker," Moss said.

"Bring it," Vivian said.

"Okay, your assertiveness when you said that really robbed me of my smug sense of superiority," Moss said.

"Maybe you should challenge her to something we all know you're really good at," Benny suggested.

"Vivian, Moss challenges you to a contest of seeing who can love our mom the most," Jessamine said.

"I'm in for poker," Giovanni said.

"Okay, but we're not going to bet with actual money this time. I'm saving up for a new sectional," Jessamine said.

"Ooh, can I buy this one when you get the new one?" Vivica asked. "Buying castoffs from Jess is the only way I can afford to outfit my house."

"Hey, why do you get dibs on the couch?" Carolyn asked. "I've known her longer. And what about Vivian?"

"Vivian's saving for a trip to Italy," Vivica said.

"You are?" Giovanni asked.

"I was," Vivian said.

"You're not anymore?" Jessamine asked.

"Maybe. I haven't thought about it much lately."

"What? That was all you talked about last summer," Vivica said. "What changed?"

"Training for a marathon takes a lot of brain power," Benny said. "Get your chips, Jess." They rearranged the living room with a table in the middle and dealt the cards while Jessamine sorted the chips.

"I'm not sure this will be enough chips for us. I should have bought another set," Jessamine said.

"We'll figure something out if we run empty," Carolyn assured her. "What are we playing?"

"Five card stud," Jessamine said. The game began with gusto but petered out until only Vivian and the Samperis were left. The remainder of the group refilled their drinks and snacks and turned on the television to await the countdown.

"I'm out," Moss said, throwing down his cards in disgust and giving up the last of his chips.

"Jess?" Benny asked.

"Raise," she called, and the game continued until she, too, called it a night and then it was only Benny, Vivian and Giovanni.

"Maybe we should make it more interesting," Giovanni said when it became clear they were all evenly matched as players.

"How so?" Vivian asked, suspicious.

"If you want to play for money, keep in mind that I've been living on rice and beans in a third world country for the past year," Benny said.

"Not money," Giovanni said. "Information."

"What exactly is it you're dying to know about me, little brother?" Benny asked.

"You're assuming you're going to win," Vivian said. "I'm still in this."

"Tough talk, library lady. Okay, what kind of information are we talking here?" Benny asked.

"The loser declares his or her biggest secret," Giovanni said. "To the group."

"Is this poker or truth or dare?" Benny asked.

"Everybody has secrets, Benny. Even you," Giovanni said. "And no one wants to give them up, so it should add an element of real fear to the game."

"I must be tired for agreeing to this, but fine. Loser spills a secret. Vivian?"

"I'm in," Vivian said, tossing another chip on the pile. In the next round, Giovanni went out on a suspiciously easy loss.

"I thought you had that one," Benny said, sounding as confused as Vivian felt.

Giovanni shrugged. "I guess it's between you two now.

Vivian resumed playing, miffed and determined to win. Was he trying to trap her into being the one to spill their secret? If so, why? So he wouldn't have to? *Nice try, but I'm not going out like that,* she thought and put renewed effort into beating Benny. In the end she did so by bluffing her face off so completely that Benny was left astounded.

"I've lost faith in humanity, Vivian. That you could lie like that to me, your brother-in-arms. I'm shocked, shocked I tell you." With a sigh, he set down his cards. "I guess you want my secret now."

"You don't have to," Vivian said. He had gotten sucked into a game of chicken between her and Giovanni and there was no need for him to become collateral damage.

"Fair is fair," he said. "My secret is that I'm so burnt out with mission work, I don't even want to look at a globe." He smiled sadly and, not for the first time, Vivian thought he looked a little lost.

"Give it time, Ben. You've only been home a little while. You might feel differently in a month or two. Maybe what you really need is some rest and healing," she suggested.

"Maybe. I'll try to keep that in mind," he said, sounding completely unconvinced.

"Life has a way of surprising you sometimes," Giovanni said. "You never know what could come along and change everything you thought you knew, in an instant and for the better."

"When did you get so wise, little brother?" Benny asked.

"August 28th," Giovanni said, and Vivian smiled because it was their wedding date.

Benny laughed. "Maybe we should do this again sometime soon," he said, his eyes on Vivian.

"Good idea, lets," Giovanni said, scooting his chair forward so he was more prominently between them.

"The countdown is getting ready to start, you guys," Jessamine called. Benny went to go sit with the group on the sectional, leaving Giovanni and Vivian by themselves at the table.

"Excellent job on the win, darling wife," Giovanni whispered. "Oh, and kudos for making my brother fall in love with you."

She rolled her eyes. "He's lonely and looking for a friend."

"He can keep looking, as far as I'm concerned," Giovanni groused.

"I'll tell Vivica the same thing," Vivian hissed.

"Huh?" Giovanni said.

"I know, Giovanni," she said.

"What do you know?" he asked.

"I know you wanted Vivica and got me by mistake," she said. It was hard to push down the tinge of hurt that crowded her throat. Giovanni made things worse by snorting a laugh so loud he had to clap his hand over his mouth. He should have been warned by the expression on Vivian's face, but instead he turned his head to watch the last few seconds of the countdown.

"Midnight," he said and leaned in for a kiss that never happened because Vivian got up and walked away. "Vivian," he called, a little too loudly because everyone turned to look at them.

"What's the problem?" Jessamine asked.

"I was attempting to kiss Vivian, and she walked away," Giovanni said. Vivian was surprised by the admission until she realized everyone in the room had kissed someone, even if it was only a peck on the cheek.

"Good job, Vivian," Carolyn said. "You've got to make them work for it."

"Vivian hasn't been kissed yet? Someone catch her and hold her still for me," Moss said.

"I'm sorry to break it to you, but not everyone in the room wants your slobbery kisses, Moss," Vivica said, scrubbing her mouth with the back of her hand. "If Giovanni's in need, however…" she let her words trail off with a flirtatious smile in his direction.

"I have to go," Vivian announced.

"So early?" Jessamine said. "You're not actually mad that Giovanni tried to kiss you, are you? Because I'm sure he was just being friendly. It's not like he's Moss and has no self-awareness."

"No, I'm getting a bit of a headache," Vivian said, which was true. She gave Jessamine a tight hug. "Thanks so much for tonight, Jess. And happy New Year."

"I'm going, too, and I'll see her out," Giovanni said. "Can you give me a ride, Vivian? I came from my parents with Moss and Benny."

"Giovanni," Jessamine said.

"It's fine, Jess. Vivian and I are pals. *Il migliore degli amici,* the best of friends, right, Vivian?"

"Right," Vivian agreed, albeit tightly. *Drat him and his Italian wooing ways.*

"*Tiene le mani a posto,*" Jessamine warned. *Keep your hands to yourself.*

"*Non posso promettertelo,*" he replied with a wink. *No promises.*

Normally Vivian would have handed him the keys and told him to drive, but tonight she wanted to be the one behind the wheel. She kept her eyes trained on the road while Giovanni darted frequent glances at her. Thankfully, he didn't try to talk until they pulled into his driveway.

"I guess I should be glad you didn't dump me on the side of the highway," he said.

"I'm upset, not psychotic," she said.

"I know, but what I don't know is why you're upset."

"Really?" she asked.

"Are you jealous? Because I can't help it if Vivica finds me irresistible. I did nothing to encourage her behavior," he said.

Vivian got out of the car, slammed into the house, and stomped up the stairs. She sat on the bed and tried to take off her boots, but the zipper was stuck.

"So this is the wrong time for humor, got it," Giovanni said. He knelt in front of Vivian and began helping her with the zipper. "Please tell me why you're angry. I promise not to tease you about it or take delight in your jealousy."

"I'm not jealous," she insisted. "Okay, I am jealous. I've never wanted to break someone's fingers before, and especially not someone I consider a friend, but you're right—it's not like Vivica knew about us."

"Are you upset about the brownies? I really was going to tell you I had them tested, eventually. But it was so fun to tease you about drugging me that I kept putting it off."

"It's not the brownies, although I can't promise I'll never be mad about that. It was a pretty rotten thing to let me wallow in my guilt over giving you tainted desserts and hornswoggling you into marrying me."

He finally got the zipper free and pulled off her boots. Still kneeling in front of her, he rested his hands on her hips. "Then what is it? Why are you mad at me?"

She shook her head, too embarrassed to tell him now that they were face to face.

"*Per favore, bella,*" he pled.

"Ugh, you've got to stop doing that. I don't even know what you're saying and it makes me give in," she said. Looking at her hands, she continued. "I was your second choice. Most of the time I try not to think about that, but seeing Vivica's perfection up close tonight, it was hard to ignore. I'm not the one you wanted, and it hurts."

"Viv," he pushed her back onto the bed and climbed up beside her. "Do you know how long I wanted Vivica instead of you? Exactly until you handed me that first brownie and said, 'Do you want to get out of here?' I had a passing attraction to a woman I didn't know and asked to be set up. I went on a date with a woman who is warm and funny and smart and lovely and I married her, not because anyone tricked me, but because I couldn't believe how good and right it felt when I was with you. And I still can't believe it. I wanted Vivica for a minute in the beginning, but *ti voglio per ora e per sempre.*"

"You have to translate that one because something tells me it was a good one," she said.

"I said I want you for now and for always. At least I think that was what I said. My verb usage is rusty. I might have said I want a vocal cat. But I think it was the first thing," he said.

"Were you really attracted to me that soon into our date?" she asked.

"I don't know how to say, 'like an out of control tire fire' in Italian, but yes," he said.

"Tire fire?"

"Now you see why I say things in Italian; they sound better," he said.

"It's incredibly unfair that you can say things in another language and I instantly forgive you," she said.

"It's incredibly unfair that you have the same effect on me by virtue of being alive," he said. "Hey, you owe me my midnight kiss."

"Never let it be said that I don't pay my debts with interest," she said.

Downstairs, an insistent knock sounded on the front door.

"Do you think it's a burglar?" Vivian asked.

"They usually prefer to ring the doorbell," Giovanni said. "I'll tell you this much, if it's one of those door-to-door cults, I'm going to join just to get rid of them. Be back in a minute, hold that thought." He put on a pair of jeans and sprinted down the stairs. Vivian wrapped a blanket around herself and hovered at the top of the stairs, ready to rush to his rescue if there was any danger.

"Hey," she heard Benny say. "I brought your car back from Mom and Dad's," followed by the sound of keys being tossed.

"Thanks."

"I'm relieved to see you. I almost thought Vivian might shove you out on the highway."

"We managed to patch things up," Giovanni said and Vivian thought it sounded like he was smiling or trying not to.

"It looks different in here," Benny said.

"Hmm, I don't think anything has changed since the last time you were here."

"It's more lived in or something." There was the sound of leather creaking, as if he sat down on the couch.

"Isn't Moss in the car?" Giovanni asked.

"He's playing with the radio," Benny said. "So, Jess has been giving me not-so-subtle hints about Vivian."

"What sort of hints?" Giovanni asked, and now it sounded as if he also sat on the couch.

"That I should ask her out, that we would be a good match. Sweet girl, Vivian."

"Come on, St. Benny, even you're not that good," Giovanni said.

"All right, when I say sweet, I mean easy on the eyes, okay?"

"I'd say that's an understatement."

"All right, she's hot. Her hair is the stuff dreams are made of, and her body..."

"Definitely stop now. Anyway, isn't she a little young for you?" Giovanni asked.

"We're adults, Giovanni. What's six years? It's not like I'm sixteen and she's ten."

"So why are you talking to me about this?" Giovanni asked.

"Because I know you went out with her," Benny said.

"You want advice?"

"I want permission. I want to know if I ask her out that we're all clear. You know, with four years between us, it's not like we've been in direct competition for dates before."

Vivian's hands were tensed on the blanket, waiting for Giovanni's answer. Would he deflect? Say yes and leave her to sort out the mess? There was a long pause, as if he was trying to decide, and then he answered.

"No, you can't have Vivian. In fact, it would be better if you stayed far away from her."

"Why?" Benny asked. Vivian wondered if the tension in his voice was from anger or confusion. Giovanni was usually a laidback sort of guy, but his answer had been anything but casual. In fact, it had sounded almost threatening.

"Because…" Giovanni began and Vivian tipped so far forward she was in danger of tumbling down the stairs. *Tell him*, she mentally urged. *Tell him we're married. Say the words and get them over with, please.* "Because I'm in love with Vivian."

She sat back and blinked. Hearing him say the words out loud, words he had never actually spoken to her, was like being handed a gift. He loved her. He *loved* her. She felt the truth of it course through her body and chided herself for being such a ninny. He was her husband, he had given her a ring, of course he loved her. But theirs hadn't been the typical courtship and hearing him say the precious words out loud felt even more wondrous than she could have imagined. She clutched the ring on the clasp around her neck. He loved her, and she loved him, and they belonged to each other. Life had never been sweeter.

"Does anyone else know?" Benny asked.

"No, and I would appreciate it if you didn't say anything." Vivian rolled her eyes, but even her irritation with his desire to keep things secret couldn't dampen the euphoria now coursing through her veins.

"She's hard to read, but I didn't get the sense she feels the same," Benny said. Vivian frowned into the darkness. Hard to read? Her? She thought she had been so obvious that she must have lit up the room.

"Then I guess I'll have to love her enough for both of us."

"Best of luck, baby brother," Benny said and Vivian smiled wryly at his dubious tone. If he only knew…It sounded as if they hugged or had some other male form of physical affection like a chest bump or some such nonsense. Then the front door opened and Giovanni was turning off the light to come back upstairs.

Vivian scrambled back to the room and jumped into bed, smoothing out the quilt to hide her flight.

"That was Benny," Giovanni said. He shimmied out of his jeans and slid into bed beside her.

"What did he want?" she asked.

"He was dropping off my car," he said.

"That was nice of him," she said.

"Good guy, Benny," he said.

"Saintly," she agreed. He had left his glasses on again. She took them off and set them on his bedside.

"Jess thinks you guys would have made a good couple," he said.

"Giovanni, if the choice was between Benny holding all the money in the world and you holding the cardboard box where we'd have to live, I would choose you and the box a thousand times over," she said. "Now, I believe I owe you a kiss."

"With interest," he reminded her.

"I'll try to make it as interesting as possible," she promised.

CHAPTER 19

The next Sunday, Vivian missed church. She had been up much of the night with a bad headache that didn't end until near dawn. When she finally fell asleep, she was in so deep that she didn't hear Giovanni leave. If not for the insistent buzzing of her phone, she might have slept several more hours. Confused, she sat up and reached for it, wondering if she had slept through school. Instead she saw a half dozen missed texts from her sister.

Where are you?

Vivian, hello?

Are you coming to church today?

Guess not. You're still coming to lunch, right?

Right? Vivian, I need to know if you're coming for lunch.

Text me back ASAP.

Vivian checked the clock and texted her sister back. If she hurried, she could just make it.

Be there in a few.

She jumped out of bed, threw on some clothes, dashed water on her face, and wound her hair into a loose bun. She texted Giovanni to let him know she was back among the land of the living.

I was going to skip family dinner to take care of you, he replied. She wondered what excuse he would have come up with to escape the mandatory weekly dinner.

I'll bank your sweetness for later so you get full credit for being thoughtful, she told him.

Now I'm going to spend the day mentally deciding what to spend my credit on, he said.

Smiling, she put away her phone and let herself into her sister's house. Annie was definitely not smiling. "Why do you look like that?" she hissed.

"The peculiar combination of our parents' DNA," Vivian said.

"You're dressed like a hobo," Annie accused.

"I was up all night with a headache. Plus I didn't know you had a formal attire requirement for lunch with family," Vivian said.

"There's someone here," Annie said.

"Is that why you're whispering? Is he holding you hostage?" Vivian said.

"He's not here for me; he's here for *you*," Annie said.

"Oh, Annie," Vivian practically wailed.

"Go make yourself presentable," Annie said, steering Vivian toward her bedroom. "Borrow whatever you want to wear and use my makeup."

Vivian was beginning to understand why Mrs. Samperi still did Giovanni's laundry. He was right—sometimes capitulation was easier. She didn't have the energy to argue with her sister. Instead she dragged herself to her room, put on her sister's too-big sweater and jeans, brushed her hair, and slapped some mineral powder on her face. *I think I looked better before,* she thought as she surveyed herself in the mirror. Annie was taller and, since the kids, heftier so that her clothes bagged on Vivian. And the bun had been preferable to her loose hair, which was now limp and hanging in her eyes. She wound it back up into the bun and left the room.

"There she is," Annie announced cheerfully as Vivian entered the room.

"Aunt Vivian," Gertrude exclaimed excitedly as she propelled herself at Vivian's legs. Vivian picked her up and covered her with kisses until she giggled. "Why are you wearing my mom's clothes?"

"Good question," Vivian said and finally turned her attention to the man Annie was attempting to present as if he were the prize pig at the fair.

"Vivian, this is Tony, he's a friend of Rob's from work. Tony, my little sister Vivian. She was up all night with a headache."

Instead of frowning at her sister like she wanted, she pasted on a smile and held out her hand for Tony to shake. "How do you do, Tony. What do you do at Rob's company?"

"I'm in human resources," Tony said. "Mostly I handle payroll and insurance. It's not interesting, but Annie tells me you're a librarian, so I guess you can relate." He laughed at his own joke and Vivian smiled weakly.

I like being a librarian, and I don't find it boring, she wanted to say, but she didn't because she didn't care about this man or his opinions. All she cared about was making it through the lunch so she could get back home to her real life. She cast about for something safe to say. "Have you worked there long?"

"About eight years. Before that I sold cars, but you can only be in sales for so long. Ten years was enough for me."

Vivian blinked at him. He had been in the working world at least eighteen years. Now that she looked closer, she could see that he was balding on top and had attempted a heroic comb over with approximately ten hairs trying to do the work of a thousand. Lines crinkled around his eyes and mouth whenever he spoke. Vivian gave Annie a look, but Annie had already deserted them to finish supper preparations.

"What about you, Vivian? Where did you work before you were at the school?" he asked.

"I was in college, and then I got my master's. This is my first grown-up job," she said.

"Wow, you're just a babe," he said, and the way he said "babe" made her think he intentionally gave it a double meaning.

"Annie, can I help you with lunch?" Vivian called.

"No, we're ready. Rob's finishing setting the table, and then we can sit."

Thank heavens for small favors, Vivian thought. At least they could eat soon, and then it would be over. But lunch dragged an interminably long time because Tony was apparently in competition to be the world's slowest eater. He would take a bite, set his fork down and talk, sip his water, take up the fork, talk some more, reach for a bite, talk again, chew the bite, set down the fork, and repeat the whole process again. After a while, Vivian gave up any pretense of trying to talk to him. She started playing a game with Gertrude and Bowden until it was time for their naps. Then she was forced to sit silently and listen while Tony and Rob talked about everyone at work as if Annie and Vivian had any idea who they were.

When Annie asked who wanted dessert, Vivian thought her head might explode. "I have to go," she said, unable to take it a minute longer.

"I should be going, too," Tony said. "There's a show on TV I don't want to miss tonight." He stood and set down his napkin, thanking Annie and Rob for lunch. "Vivian, it was a pleasure to meet you. Can I walk you to your car?"

He had that look, the one that said he would try to kiss her if she left the house alone with him. "I'm not going out yet, thanks. I have to change my clothes. You go ahead. It was nice to meet you, have a nice evening." She sat with a determined smile until he finally left.

"That was kind of rude," Annie said when he was gone.

"Rude? Rude is ambushing someone for a set up they in no way wanted or requested. Where are you getting these men? And does their pensioner's home know they've been kidnapped?"

"Is it because he's bald?" Annie asked.

"No, I have no trouble with baldness. I would, however, like a man young enough to have a functioning prostate," Vivian said.

"Sex isn't everything in marriage," Annie said.

"I'm only twenty-six years old. Please give me a few years of being a newlywed to figure that out on my own," Vivian said.

"I want to see you settled. I want to see you with someone."

"And you think it's going to be one of these boring old men?" Vivian asked.

"I know you."

"Here we go with that again."

"You'll never get there. No one will ever be good enough or settled enough or *something* enough, so I'm bringing you men who are already mature and settled," Annie said.

"No offense, Annie, but that's like the cat equivalent of bringing me a dead mouse for supper and then being offended when I don't eat it. I don't want to be set up. Please, stop."

"It's not like our town is overflowing with single young men on the prowl," Annie said.

"If you never say 'on the prowl' again, this day will not have been wasted," Vivian said.

"Why don't you join one of those dating sites," Annie suggested.

Vivian put her head in her hands. What she wouldn't give to tell her sister the truth right now. She put her head up. What if there was a way she could have it both ways? She could say enough to get Annie off her back without compromising Giovanni's precious privacy. "I have found someone, someone I'm interested in."

"Really? Who?" Annie leaned forward as if she was about to receive the secret of life.

"Giovanni Samperi."

Annie's face recoiled into a grimace so fast she probably created stretch marks. "One of the Samperis?"

"What's wrong with the Samperis? You know Jessamine is one of my closest friends."

If possible, Annie's expression became even sourer. "How can you be friends with her? She's such a snob."

"No she isn't."

"Yes, she is. You're forgetting she and I were in the same grade. She was in with the mean, popular rich kids. Miss homecoming princess who was too good for everybody else."

"You make it sound like we went to school in *The Outsiders*. It's not like we were poor or lacking in any way."

"Still, she wasn't nice, and neither were her friends, Carolyn and all those other stuck ups."

"That doesn't sound anything like Jessamine," Vivian said.

"Maybe you don't know her well enough yet," Annie said.

"Maybe you're the one who doesn't know her. Did you ever actually talk to her?"

"As if she would have given me or my geek friends the time of day."

"What do you have against Giovanni?"

"He was a couple of years behind me, but I could tell he was the same way. He thought he was better than everyone, so standoffish. All of the Samperis are snobs."

"They are not. They are delightfully kind and warm, and they've given tons of money to various causes around town."

"Showing off, you mean," Annie said.

"This is bringing out a lovely color in you," Vivian said. "Setting aside the ancient history of high school, what possible objection could you have to Giovanni?"

"I don't think it's a good match. It would never work between you, even if he was interested."

"Why not?"

"All I'm saying is not to get your hopes up," Annie said.

"How did I survive our childhood with my self-esteem intact?" Vivian wondered aloud.

"Don't get all huffy, Vivian. You know I'm a realist. You're very pretty, but Giovanni looks like the type of guy who is into his looks and wants to be with someone who is into hers. He probably drives a sports car and hangs out in bars all night. That's not you."

She could argue, but she didn't want to. Someday the truth would out and Annie would have to eat her words. Until then Vivian would keep on keeping on. "Let's agree to disagree, but please, please no more fix-ups."

"I'm out of men, anyway," Annie said, sounding deflated. Upstairs Bowden began to cry. "Naptime's over."

Vivian volunteered to clean up while Annie retrieved the kids. By the time she got home, it was suppertime. Giovanni was waiting for her in the kitchen with a plate full of shrimp scampi and a cannoli. "Ta-da! I wrestled Moss for the last cannoli and smuggled it to you."

Vivian bypassed the heaping plate of food and jumped into his embrace, forcing him to catch her one-handed. "What's wrong?" he asked.

"My sister tried to set me up again." She buried her nose against his neck and inhaled.

"Not a love match?"

"His name was Tony Rogers."

"So?"

"So in case you're keeping track, Annie has now tried to set me up with Mr. McGregor, Pee Wee Herman, and Mr. Rogers. If she knew someone in the military, I'd probably be going on a date with Captain Kangaroo any minute now," she said.

He laughed and set the plate aside so he could hold her with both hands. "Vivian, you make me laugh."

She let him go and sat down to polish off the cannoli. "Did you know Annie in school?"

"What year was she in?" he asked.

"Jessamine's class."

"No, I don't remember her. Were she and Jess friends?"

"No."

"Figures. Jess didn't hang with the nicest crowd. We didn't like any of her friends. Carolyn's the only one who lingered."

"Did you enjoy high school?" she asked.

"Not really," he said.

"Why not?"

"Square peg, round hole. I wasn't into the party scene, and I worked a lot."

"You worked during high school?"

"My dad believed the best way to keep a kid out of trouble was to keep him busy. We all started learning the trade when we were fourteen. I worked most evenings and weekends, so there wasn't much time for sports or other activities."

"Do you regret that?" she asked.

"No, I like to work and I'm not incredibly social. And I was with all my siblings who are my best friends, present company excluded."

She smiled as she licked powdered sugar off her fingers. "Did you ever own a sports car?"

"Every guy wants a sports car at some point in his life, but I realized fairly early I'm more of a sedan type person," he said. "What's this about, Vivy? Are you hinting you'd like to buy a sports car?"

"No, I'm trying to get to know you better."

He tipped his head. "You know me better than anyone."

She smiled. "Yes, I suppose that's true. And you know what, Giovanni?"

"What, Vivian?"

"I love you. I love, love, love you." She kissed him, and he responded in kind. "You know what else I love?"

"Hmm," he said.

"Your lack of age spots and highly-functioning prostate."

"Huh?"

"Never mind. Please pass the scampi."

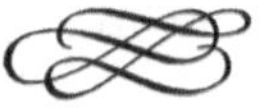

CHAPTER 20

Over the next few weeks, Vivian and Giovanni saw less and less of each other. The spring thaw meant Vivian had to train harder than ever for the marathon, while warmer weather meant more work for Giovanni.

"Do you think we'll ever get another winter this perfect again?" Vivian fretted. Somehow it had felt as if they were alone in the world. The fact that no one knew about them, combined with all the time they spent at home together, made it seem as if they were isolated from the world.

"We'll make it so," Giovanni promised. "Winter will be our time."

It still feels like winter today, Vivian thought as she started on her ninth mile of the day. Ironically, Evan had dropped out of their training partnership because of his wife's complaints.

"You're not married," he had told Vivian. "You don't know what it's like to have a jealous wife. Sorry, Vivian."

"I understand," Vivian had told him. "Do what you need to do to make your marriage work." For a minute, she had contemplated dropping out of the marathon, but she had already registered, and she had already come so far. She was enjoying running. And after so much of Mama Samperi's pasta and cannoli, she needed the exercise.

As she neared the end of her run, she hit a patch of black ice and went down hard, splaying her hands out in front of her to break the fall. She lay on her stomach for a minute, catching her breath and attempting to assess the damage. Nothing was broken, that was good news. But when she attempted to get up, her ankle protested mightily. Thankfully she was only a quarter mile from home. She pulled out her phone and called Giovanni, glad he was home early for once.

"I fell," she said. "Can you come get me?"

He was there in two minutes, scooping her off the sidewalk and into the warm car. "Are you all right? Do you need to go to the hospital?"

"I really don't," she said. "I'm hoping I only wrenched it a little. I can't afford to take time off when I'm so close to the end."

"My poor Vivy," he said as he helped her limp into the living room. He settled her onto the couch and examined her ankle.

"Do you have any idea what you're looking for?" she asked, amused at his proprietary ministrations.

"No, but no bones are sticking out, so that's probably a good thing," he said. "You know what you need?"

"A cannoli?" she said.

"Horse liniment."

"Does that taste like cannoli?"

"You don't eat it; you rub it on your ankle. I knew this guy who trained horses and he swore by it. My mom kept some in the house for our various injuries. And you know us, there were a lot of injuries."

"I don't have any," she said because it was the weekend and they were at her house.

"I do. I'll run to my house and get it," he said. "Don't move until I get back." He kissed her and let himself out. A minute later, she heard the car drive away and the doorbell rang.

Hobbling, she made her way to the door. "Jessamine," she exclaimed.

"Why are you bent over?" Jessamine asked.

"I fell and wrenched my ankle."

"Here, let me help you," Jessamine said. She slipped an arm around Vivian's waist and helped her back to the couch.

"Better?" Jessamine asked as she arranged the blanket over Vivian.

"Yes, thank you."

"Did I just see Giovanni drive away from here?" Jessamine asked.

"Did you?" Vivian asked.

"In your car," Jessamine added.

"Um…" Vivian stalled.

"And you're wearing his sweatshirt and a tidy stack of his underwear is in your laundry basket," Jessamine said. She sat heavily in the opposing wing chair. "What's going on, Vivian? Are you dating my brother?"

Vivian twisted her fingers together nervously in her lap. "Maybe you should ask him about that."

"I'm asking you," Jessamine said and Vivian suddenly understood why construction workers looked up to her as their boss. Her tone brooked no refusal.

"We're married," Vivian blurted before clapping her hands over her mouth.

Jessamine's mouth, however, was wide open. For a long time no sound came out, and then she shouted. "What? I mean, I thought maybe you guys had a thing going on New Year's, but this, this is… when did this happen?"

"In August, on our first date," Vivian said. She felt weak and light-headed. Any minute Giovanni was going to come back and find out she had blurted their secret to his family. How angry would he be?

Jessamine blinked at her. "I don't know whether to hug you or punch you."

"I'm sorry, Jess, really I am. But Giovanni wants to keep it secret."

"Why?" Jessamine yelled.

"Because of your family," Vivian said.

"What's wrong with my family?" Jessamine yelled, and now she was standing toweringly over Vivian.

"Nothing," Vivian hastened to say, trying not to cower. "I love your family. I love *you*. I think Giovanni seems to think we wouldn't have any privacy, that people would be too involved in our business."

"That's a given," Jessamine said. Sounding less angry, she sat back down. "Sorry if I scared you."

"I had it coming. I don't like keeping things from you, especially not things of this magnitude."

"You're really married? Like conjugal visit married?"

Vivian nodded. "We split our time between houses."

"I guess that explains why he's never home when I stop over," Jessamine said. "How's it going? I mean, is it a good thing that you're married?"

"I don't have words to tell you how good it is," Vivian said, and the hint of a smile appeared on Jessamine's lips.

"Always remember it was me who set you up."

"You could give my sister a few pointers," Vivian said.

"So, I guess the cat's out of the bag now. Mom is going to freak."

"No," Vivian said.

"What do you mean no?"

"I mean I didn't have Giovanni's permission to tell you."

"What is this, 1950?"

"No, but you know how private he is. Things are so, so good between us right now, Jess. I don't want to do anything to upset him. When we tell your family, I want it to be a mutual decision. I don't think he's there yet."

"And where are you?" Jessamine asked.

"Ready to shout it from the rooftops," Vivian said.

"Vivian, keeping a secret like this isn't normal. Doesn't it bother you?"

Vivian shrugged.

"This is so stupid, and it's all Giovanni's fault. You know why this is? It's because he's never had to work for anything before. Good grades, family job, wife…it all was handed to him on a platter. You know what you need to do? You need to make him come out into the open, like force him into a public declaration or something," Jessamine said.

"No, Jess, please. That's not us, and it's not what I want, either. Please, please, please can you go back to pretending you don't know? And please, please, please don't tell your family. Giovanni would be so upset if they found out from someone other than him."

Jessamine sighed. "For you, I'll keep the secret. But I want it on the record I think this is really stupid and unhealthy."

"Duly noted," Vivian said. "Hey, not to sound rude, but what are you doing here? I'm thrilled to see you, but it's not your usual M/O to drop by."

Jessamine grinned. "I heard from the TV show. They said yes."

Vivian squealed. "I would so stand up and hug you right now, if I could. That is so exciting. Congratulations!"

Jessamine laughed. "You're the one who got married, why are you congratulating me? We both need congratulated. And, hey, you're my sister-in-law now."

"The perks of this marriage thing keep getting better and better," Vivian said.

"What does your family think?"

"I haven't told them yet," Vivian said.

Jessamine groaned. "Do not let my brother keep you under his thumb. Seriously, Vivian, you have to take a stand."

"I'll consider it."

Jessamine left soon after. Vivian could tell she wanted to stay and confront Giovanni, but, for Vivian's sake, she didn't.

Giovanni returned a few minutes after his sister left. "Give me your foot," he commanded. He poured some strong-smelling blue liquid in his hand and rubbed it on her ankle. Vivian watched him work, wondering if she should confess the truth about Jessamine's visit. Before she could come to any sort of conclusion, Giovanni had finished with her ankle and was now washing his hands. After he was finished, he heated supper and brought it to her on a tray.

"I should wrench my ankle every day," she said.

"Then you wouldn't be able to do your marathon," he said. "Is your sister going to watch you run?"

"Only if they're giving away a million dollars at the finish line.

Although I guess I could ask her. It might be worth it to hear her reaction if I suggested she wake at four in the morning, drive an hour, and stand in the cold while I run a few hours." Now that she thought about it, she wasn't sure Giovanni would want to attend either. Being a spectator at a marathon was more an act of love than a fun outing. "You don't have to go," she hastily added.

"You don't want me there?"

"Of course I want you there, but I don't want you to feel obligated. It'll be a long day," she said.

"I was thinking about that. What if we went the night before and got a hotel room? We could go out to eat. You could carb load," he said.

They could have a real date; they could be seen in public together. "I would love that," she said emphatically.

"What about Evan?" he asked.

"It would probably be a little awkward if he tagged along, but I could ask him, if you like," she said.

"I meant is it going to be weird if you don't go with him after you've intermittently trained together?"

"I can't imagine why it would be," she said.

They finished eating. Giovanni cleared their plates and tidied the kitchen. Until that moment, she hadn't realized that they had assumed traditional gender roles in their relationship. On most nights Vivian prepared supper and cleaned up afterward, even when they were at his house. In so many ways they had slipped seamlessly into their marriage, but even though it felt traditional, it wasn't. Their households were still separate, as were their finances. When Vivian wasn't there, she didn't keep so much as a toothbrush at his house, and the same was true for him when he was at her house.

What would Jessamine think of that? Vivian wondered. If she had freaked out over their secrecy, what would she think of the absolute division between certain aspects of their lives? For that matter, why were they so divided? Vivian had no idea how much Giovanni made, how much he had in the bank, if he had a retirement plan, or if his car was paid off. How was it that she could take her clothes off in front of him without a thought but turned chicken at the idea of discussing his 401K?

She should tell him Jessamine knew their secret, but it was one more reality she wasn't ready to confront. Not only did she not want to spoil their night, but knowing Jessamine knew made everything feel a little bit different. How would it feel when everyone knew? Was part of the magic of their relationship due to the secrecy?

Vivian didn't enjoy confrontation. She preferred to let sleeping dogs lie, as her grandmother would say. But how long could they reasonably ignore the pertinent issues between them until things came to a head? Not long, as it turned out.

CHAPTER 21

The weekend of the marathon was perfect weather for running. Giovanni and Vivian felt giddy as they loaded up his car and headed out of town.

"Do we have everything?" Vivian asked. No matter how many lists she made, she always felt as if she was forgetting something.

"One more thing," Giovanni said. He reached for her necklace, took the ring off, and slid it on her finger. "Now it's official."

Vivian held out her hand to inspect it. They had been married for more than eight months, and this would mark the first time she wore her ring in public. "Could you wear a ring?" she asked.

"What do you mean by 'could'?" he asked.

"You work in construction. Is it a job hazard?"

"Joe wears one, and he still has all his digits," he said.

She wanted to see her ring on his hand, to have a physical symbol of belonging and possession. But currently she lacked the funds to do anything more than fashion tinfoil into a circle and wrap it around his finger. She certainly didn't have the money to buy him a matching platinum band. With the sad state of her finances, it was doubtful she ever would.

"Are you nervous about tomorrow?" he asked.

"A little," she admitted. She had only run thirteen miles twice in the last month, and it had been more exhausting than she expected. "I'm hoping the adrenaline of the event will carry me through."

"You'll do fine," he assured her.

His words had the opposite effect of making her more nervous. Up to this point, the marathon had only been about her, but now Giovanni was involved, if only as a spectator. What if she didn't make it? She would feel embarrassed, as if she were letting him down.

Her phone rang and she answered it without thinking. "Hello."

"Hello, pretty girl," Evan chirped.

Giovanni gave her a sideways frown. She shrugged. Evan hadn't talked to her that way in months, since the beginning of the school year.

"Do you want to meet for supper tonight?" Evan asked.

"I'm going out of town," Vivian said.

He paused. "The night before the marathon?"

She almost blurted that she was heading to the race early to get a hotel room, but a sudden sense of foreboding stopped her. She had a premonition that if she gave him that news, he would suggest coming with her.

"I'll make it there on time," she said.

"I think we should set up a meeting place so we can find each other. They're expecting a few thousand entrants. I looked on the map and there's a statue of Mingus Bird. We could meet there."

"Who's Mingus Bird?" she asked.

"I have no idea. Nice name, though."

"That's a matter of opinion. The meeting place sounds good. I'll see you tomorrow."

"See you tomorrow," Evan said, his tone a little too chipper and intimate for Vivian's taste. And Giovanni's too, if the look he gave her was any indication.

"How's Evan?" he asked.

"He's acting strangely. I promise, he has not been acting like that at school. I thought he was getting back together with his wife."

"He has a lot of issues, that guy. Why is he taking them out on you?

And does he really expect you to be there waiting on the sidelines for him to emerge from the broken ruins of his marriage? How desperate does he think you are?" Giovanni said.

"I never thought of it that way. It's interesting to hear things from the male perspective. What else can you teach me about men?" she asked.

"That they don't like to share," he said, reaching for her hand. It was the first time they had been in a car together since New Year's.

How odd, Vivian thought. That she had been more intimate with this man than with anyone and yet had barely ever ridden in the same vehicle with him was one more quirk in their already quirky arrangement. "You held my hand the night we got married, do you remember?" she asked. "After we left the last dance club, before we went to Gatlinburg."

"And then you kissed me."

"You most definitely kissed me," she said.

"That's not how I remember it. I was young and naïve and you sliced through my innocence like a hot knife on butter. What else could I do but marry you after that?" he said.

"What if you hadn't?" she asked.

"What do you mean?"

"What if we hadn't gotten married that night? Would I ever have heard from you again?" she asked.

"I would like to say something romantic, like we were meant to be. But the reality is that I probably would have found a way to talk myself out of it. I would have blamed it on the night or the brownies or something. I don't have a history of taking leaps, especially when it comes to people. But I also think that was why I took the leap that night, because some part of me realized it was now or never and I wanted it to be now." He glanced at her profile. "You're quiet. Did I hurt your feelings? Should I say something clever in Italian?"

"No, I'm not upset. I was trying to imagine what I would have done if we had gone our separate ways that night."

"What would you have done?" he asked.

"I like to imagine I would have done something dramatic, like move somewhere exotic, like maybe try to work at the Library of Congress. In reality I probably would have stuffed my feelings aside and tried to seem aloof whenever we met."

"It's amazing that a couple of risk takers like us wound up together," he said.

"No regrets?" she asked.

"Only that we didn't meet in high school. We could have been one of those couples, like Joe and Peaches, who meet as kids and stay together forever."

"That was sweet and romantic and you didn't even say it in Italian," she said.

"Every once in a while I get it right," he said.

"I'd say more than every once in a while," she said.

They arrived at the hotel, changed clothes, and went back out again. Giovanni had made reservations at a swanky steakhouse under the name "Mr. and Mrs. Samperi." No one made reservations that way anymore, but Vivian and Giovanni didn't care. When their names were finally called, they had to fight the urge to stand and yell, "That's us, we're Mr. and Mrs. Samperi!"

After supper, they went to a movie.

"I shouldn't be staying up this late," Vivian said as she crawled into bed beside Giovanni and turned on the television. Neither of them had a TV in their bedrooms, and watching from bed felt like a luxury.

"I predict you'll be asleep within ten minutes," Giovanni said.

"You're probably right," she said sleepily. She handed him the remote, pillowed her head on his chest, and was out in eight minutes.

Despite the late night, she felt a buzz of energized excitement when she woke at four the next morning. This was the day she had been training for for months. She felt ready, more ready than she had in days. Giovanni deposited her at registration and went to wait with the other spectators.

She kissed him. "Thanks for being here, it means the world to me. I'll see you in a few hours."

"Run well or whatever you say to runners. Don't break a leg, maybe?" he said.

With a final wave, he disappeared. Vivian wended her way through the crowd to meet Evan. There was a not-so-small part of her that hoped he wouldn't be there, but he was at the assigned place, one arm braced on the statue while he stretched.

"Hey, you made it," he said. He let go the statue to give her a one-armed hug that she practically squirmed out of.

"Hi. Listen, I've been meaning to tell you not to try and keep pace with me. I know you're a faster runner. It won't bother me if you go on ahead. I'm sure we'll touch base at the finish," she said.

He seemed hesitant. "Well, if you're sure. I don't want to ditch you, but I'm trying to beat my personal record."

"So am I, but yours is still a lot faster," she said.

Nearby, an official whistled and it was time to line up. She and Evan high fived for luck, the starting pistol went off, and the race began.

It took Vivian about a quarter of a mile to get into a groove and settle into the right pace. She blamed nerves and the jostling crowd of runners. By the time she began to settle into her pace, the crowd around her began to thin. Faster runners, like Evan, went on ahead. Slower runners and walkers lagged behind. A quick peek at her fellow mid-pacers revealed a few older gentlemen and a couple of other women about her age.

While she ran, she tried not to think of much at all. Deep thoughts were too distracting, but if she didn't focus on something, her mind began to drift, dangerously altering her pace. Instead she settled on a kind of background white noise—replaying old movie quotes or flicking through the mental catalogue of her favorite books and authors. When her thoughts strayed to Giovanni, she yanked them back again. He was most definitely not white noise and too distracting for her much-needed mental energy.

She didn't allow herself to think of him until around mile ten when her energy began to lag and her body started to ache. Her mind grew weary and started to tell her she couldn't finish. She was tempted to slow down, possibly even to walk the remaining three miles. But she knew Giovanni was waiting for her at the end and, while he might be proud of ten miles, he would be prouder still of a completed race, a goal reached. So she allowed her thoughts to linger on him as she pushed through the last three grueling miles.

He must have been watching for her because when Vivian stepped over the half-marathon finish point, Giovanni was waiting for her. She kept her eyes trained on him as she hurried forward. Despite the fact that she was sweaty and stinky gross, she wanted nothing more than to throw her arms around him and feel his arms around her.

Instead a different pair of arms circled her waist and pulled her up. Before she could comprehend what was happening, Evan had picked her up and pressed his lips to hers for a kiss. And then Giovanni was there, tapping him on the shoulder.

"I'm afraid I'm going to need you to let go of my wife."

CHAPTER 22

The ride home was awkward, more awkward than their first date, mostly because they weren't speaking.

After Evan had let her go, his face flushing with embarrassment and surprise, Vivian hadn't known what to say.

"I told you things were complicated," she offered lamely before Giovanni took her hand and led her away.

"I'm so sorry," she said to Giovanni as soon as they were out of earshot.

"It wasn't your fault," he said, but he sounded terse. And that was the last thing he said. He remained silent while they drove back to the hotel for their things, and now he was silent on the drive home.

Vivian was similarly quiet. Somehow she sensed the easy intimacy and camaraderie between them was gone, possibly forever. Something happened to Giovanni when Evan kissed her, something more than jealousy. She had no idea what it was and therefore had no idea how to fix it. So she sat in worried silence and let him stew.

Three times during the long afternoon, she tried to broach the subject, but Giovanni brushed her off. By the evening, she was feeling vexed herself. "I'm going to my book group," she announced.

He nodded without looking up from his book. She grabbed her

keys and purse and slammed from the house. All she wanted was an evening away and a chance for both of them to cool down. Instead she got Jessamine and her overly-eager curiosity.

"What's wrong, Vivian?" Jessamine whispered during a lull in the book club discussion. Vivian shook her head. "Is it my brother?" Vivian shrugged. Jessamine sat back and crossed her arms, pinning Vivian with an intense frown.

When the meeting was over, everyone left except Vivian and Jessamine. "Seriously, what's going on with you?" Jessamine tried again.

"It's nothing," Vivian said.

"Vivian, you're a Samperi now. That means you're not allowed to keep anything to yourself; it's the law. What's up with you and Giovanni? Did you have a fight?"

"I don't know," Vivian wailed. Maybe it would help to discuss the situation. "This morning was my marathon."

"How did it go?"

"Really well. Giovanni and I went early and had an amazing time. But then after the race Evan kissed me."

"And Giovanni got jealous. Did he hit him?" She sounded absurdly hopeful that he had.

"Of course not. But he hasn't spoken to me since," Vivian said.

"Why? It wasn't your fault."

"I know. I don't know what's going on."

"I think we need to go back to my original plan."

"What was your original plan?" Vivian asked with no small amount of trepidation. Jessamine had the look, the same one she got when talking about removing support beams and rearranging plumbing from one side of a house to another. No scheme was too grand when she had a plan.

"Here's what we're going to do: As soon as school is out, you're going to go to Italy. You can stay with my Zia, my grandma's sister. We won't tell Giovanni where you went. He'll have to find you; he'll have to come and get you. And he'll have to tell everyone where he's going and why."

"I don't think…" Vivian began, but Jessamine interrupted her.

"It's the perfect plan. You can see Italy while staying with family, Giovanni will have to get over himself and make a grand gesture, and the stupid secret will be out of the bag."

"I'm sure your aunt is a lovely woman, and you know I want to see Italy, but I don't want to go by myself. And I don't want to leave Giovanni."

"You wouldn't be leaving him forever, just for a couple of weeks until he figures out where you've gone."

"What if he never figured it out?" Vivian asked.

"Eventually I'd tell him," Jessamine assured her.

Vivian saw endless faults with the plan, but Jessamine wasn't willing to take no for an answer. And since they had a couple of weeks until school was out, she let her talk, nodding meekly when appropriate.

Later, she let herself into her house, not sure what to expect. Would Giovanni still be there or would he have gone home? To her relief, she found him lying asleep in her bed. She turned on the lamp and perched on his side of the bed. Groggily, he opened his eyes and peered at her.

"I think your sister is planning to kidnap me."

Of all the things she could have said, that was what he least expected. He sat up and rubbed his eyes. "What?"

Vivian let out a breath. Where to begin? "Giovanni, I have no interest in Evan, I've never had any interest in Evan. I've never encouraged him. In fact, I discouraged him and told him I wasn't interested. A few times."

"I know that, Vivian."

"Then why did you get so mad at me?" she asked.

"I wasn't mad at you. I was upset with the situation. I guess I didn't handle it so well," he said. "The truth is, I'm really tired of this."

"Of me? Of our marriage?" she tried not to let it, but her voice betrayed her with a quaver.

His eyes widened. "No, of course not. How could you think that? I meant I'm tired of all the secrecy. I know you're a private person and your relationship with your family is tricky, but I'm tired of sneaking around. This weekend showed me how much. I want to go public. I want to leave the house with my wife and be able to call her my wife."

"But you're the one who wanted to keep it a secret for so long," she exclaimed. "You're private and you didn't want your family to find out."

"No, I kept it a secret for you," he said.

They were silent a few beats while their words caught up with them. "Wow, are we stupid or what?" he finally said.

"Stupid's a strong word. Ignorant, maybe, and really bad at communication," she said.

He took her hand, the one still wearing his ring. "All this time you wanted to let the cat out of the bag?"

"I wanted to set the cat's paw prints on the Hollywood walk of fame and televise the event," she said.

"Huh?"

"I wanted everyone to know," she clarified. "I wanted to shout it from the rooftops."

"Me, too," he said. He reached for her and pulled her into his lap. How she longed to stop the discussion right there, to celebrate and make up. Instead she put up her hand.

"There's something else I have to tell you," she said.

"You're already secretly married to someone else," he guessed.

"Worse." She swallowed and forced the difficult words through her swollen throat. "I'm in debt. Huge, raging, big-time debt, from which I'll probably never recover. It's not credit card debt," she hastened to add. "It's school loans, and a car loan, and my mortgage. But still, it's a lot." She took a breath, not daring to look at him. "I'm sorry I didn't tell you earlier. I guess I was embarrassed, and I didn't know how."

He slid out from beneath her and left the room. Stunned, she sat still for a few minutes, willing the tears to go back into their wells. When they did, she eased out of bed and stumbled down the hall in search of Giovanni. If he thought he could walk away so easily after they had just made up, he had another think coming.

She found him sitting at the kitchen table, her tidy financial portfolio sprawled before him. "What are you doing?" she asked.

"I should have looked at this thing ages ago. I didn't want to intrude," he said. "I could have helped. Is this why you never buy anything?"

"I'm on a tight budget," she said.

"Vivian, Vivian, Vivian," he sighed. "Why didn't you tell me?"

"Maybe because every time I tell you something you disappear and go into another room," she said, irritated. Was he angry with her or not? She still wasn't certain.

"My mind runs ahead of my mouth most of the time. I think things through and then I respond," he replied absently as his finger traced down the page of her most private financial information. "Here we go."

"What is it?" she asked, impatience creeping into her tone.

"Sit down," he said. When she sat in the chair beside him, he rolled his eyes and pulled her into his lap again. "My house was a repo because it was a hovel. I bought it cheap, paid it off, and did my own renovations. I own it outright."

Was he trying to make her feel worse about her situation? If so, he was succeeding. "Okay," she drawled.

"My point is that it wouldn't make sense to sell my house. I think we should sell yours and use the equity to pay off your car. No offense, but we don't really need your salary to survive. If we put all of it toward the school debt, you can have it paid off in three to four years."

In reply, Vivian burst into tears.

"*Bella*, we don't have to," Giovanni soothed. "We could keep your house and rent mine, if you want."

"I don't care about the house," she said between great, heaving sobs. "I'm so relieved. I thought I would never, ever get out of debt. This weight has been sitting on my chest since college, getting worse and worse every year. And now you're offering me a way out, and you make it sound so simple. And we're going to live together in one house like real married people."

"So, you're happy," he said slowly.

She nodded, both hands fisted over her now-swollen eyes.

"Happy tears are completely confusing for a guy," he said. "There's one more thing, though." His tone was so grave that she uncovered her eyes and looked at him.

"What?"

"Someone's going to have to tell my mother we're married," he said.

CHAPTER 23

They stayed up most of the night talking and planning. Between the exhaustion and the relief, Vivian felt almost light headed. And they still had to go to Samperi Sunday and spill the beans. But there was one thing Vivian had to do first.

Her fingers shook a little as she pushed the button for Annie's number. Her sister answered on the first ring.

"What's wrong?" she asked.

"Why do you always assume something is wrong?" Vivian asked.

"Because it's eight o'clock on a Sunday morning and you hate waking up early," Annie said.

"I'm finally ready to talk about Gatlinburg."

It sounded like Annie sat down. "I'm listening."

"You were right when you said something happened."

"I knew it. Was it a man?" Annie asked.

"It was."

"Was it that Samperi guy?" Annie said.

"How did you know?" Vivian said.

"Lucky guess. He used you and then he left you stranded there and you've been wasting away for him ever since. That's it, isn't it? I told you those Samperis were no good."

"Not exactly."

"Well, then what is it?" Annie said.

So Vivian told her, and Annie screamed so loud she had to hold the phone away from her ear. She covered the mouthpiece and whispered to Giovanni. "Do you want French toast?"

He nodded. "Do you want me to make it?"

"I'll do it. This could go on for a while." She set the phone down and made breakfast while Annie's admonishing screeches rattled in the background. When breakfast was finished and Annie was all yelled out, she came around, offering Vivian her heartfelt congratulations and inviting Giovanni for lunch.

"I'll bring him around soon, but not today. Today we tell the Samperis," Vivian said and a little burble of queasiness rattled through her gut.

"Should I pray for you?" Annie joked. In the background, Giovanni nodded, and he wasn't joking.

By the time they cleaned up breakfast and showered, it was too late for church. Vivian lingered in the bathroom, making sure her hair was perfect. At last Giovanni came to retrieve her.

"We have to go; we'd best not put it off any longer." He said it in the same tone one might use when heading to the gallows. Silently, Vivian trooped behind him to the car.

They entered the house together, miraculously unseen, and made their way to the kitchen. Mama Samperi had her back to them but seemed to sense Giovanni's presence because she spoke.

"You missed church this morning, son," she said. "Are you sick?"

"No, Ma, sorry. It was a late night and we decided to sleep in."

She nodded and resumed working with her back to them. Vivian gave Giovanni a questioning look. "Wait for it," he whispered and, sure enough, Mrs. Samperi's head rose. Her back straightened, and she turned.

"What do you mean 'we' decided to sleep in?" she asked.

"Vivian and I. We decided to sleep in this morning."

"Pete, get in here," Mrs. Samperi yelled.

"Marie, the game's on," Mr. Samperi yelled.

"Pete," she replied and the game came to an abrupt halt as the other family members began to filter in. "Continue, Giovanni."

"I was saying that Vivian and I had a late night last night, so we decided to sleep in this morning."

Beside them, Moss snickered.

"And why was Vivian at your house?" Mrs. Samperi asked.

"Technically I was at Vivian's house because it was Saturday and we stay at her house on the weekends. Because we live together."

"Pete, are you hearing this?" Mrs. Samperi yelled.

"I'm right here, Marie. Boy, you'd better elaborate because the vein in your mother's neck is starting to pulse."

"The thing is, Ma, Vivian and I, we're married." He held up Vivian's hand and showed his mother the ring. "Surprise."

"Pete!"

"I heard, Marie. When did this happen?"

"August 28th," Giovanni said. Beside them, Moss snickered again.

"What?" Joe said. "You got married on your first date?"

"I told you I didn't reject her," Giovanni said.

"You also told me you kept it casual," Jessamine said.

"It was a casual ceremony," Giovanni assured her. To his left, Joe started to laugh, and then Benny.

"Do you mean to tell me you have been secretly married and cohabitating for the last eight months?" Mrs. Samperi asked.

"Closer to nine," Giovanni said and at that the remaining members of the family cracked and started to chuckle, all except Mrs. Samperi who stepped out of her heels.

"Son, you'd better pray you can outrun me because only Jesus can save you now," she said as she reached for the largest wooden spoon from the crock on her counter. Giovanni smiled uncertainly at her until Moss gave him a little push toward the door and said, "Run, *stupido*."

For an older woman, Mrs. Samperi was fast. She took off after her fourth born like a whiz-bang, pausing only at the door to point her spoon at Vivian and say, "You're next, young lady," before sprinting out the door.

"If the sauce burns, I bet he gets double," Moss said and then the tension was broken and everyone fell to congratulating Vivian, picking her up and hugging her before passing her to the next in line.

"Sister Vivian, indeed," Benny said with a smile and a kiss on the cheek before handing her off to Moss who kissed her full on the lips.

"Moss," she said, shoving him hard in the chest.

"I had to say goodbye to all we could have had together," Moss insisted.

"Good thing Giovanni didn't see or you would have to say goodbye to your life," Joe said dryly.

When Giovanni and his mother returned, they were arm in arm and smiling, although she did still swat Vivian on the behind with her spoon before drawing her into a tight hug and kissing both cheeks.

"Welcome to the Samperis," Mr. Samperi boomed.

"Good luck," Peaches said quietly to her right. "You're going to need it."

*Thank you for reading *A Secret Foundation.* For more books, please visit my website www.vanessagraybartal.com